Letters from
Pleasant View Lutheran Church

Christmas 1985 to Christmas 1999

Dave Alan Nerdig

Order this book online at www.trafford.com
or email orders@trafford.com

Most Trafford titles are also available at major online book retailers.

Printed in the United States of America.

ISBN: 978-1-4907-1392-2 (sc)
ISBN: 978-1-4907-1391-5 (hc)
ISBN: 978-1-4907-1393-9 (e)

Library of Congress Control Number: 2013916601

Trafford rev. 05/30/2014

 www.trafford.com

North America & international
toll-free: 1 888 232 4444 (USA & Canada)
fax: 812 355 4082

To my loving wife, Linda.
After thirty-five years, she is still laughing.
What a lucky man I am.

Contents

Jack Jonas: Shepherd of the Flock

December 25, 1985

Michael Loeson was excited about the shepherds. He wasn't out of seminary a year yet, and he was about to preach his first Christmas sermon. In November, he accepted a call to a tiny country parish in South Dakota. Its white-framed church building was planted smack-dab in the middle of a snow swept wheat field. His call committee kidded him, "Well, it's not the end of the world, but you can see it from here." He wanted to impress his parish. As the new kid on the block, he wanted to relate personally to them, to be one of them. He wanted to prove to them that they made the right choice choosing him. So he took down his commentaries and began to read everything he could about sheep and shepherds and the way the religious types of Jesus's day felt about them. He was a city boy, but he found it invigorating to saturate himself in such an agrarian topic.

On behalf of his parishioners, he felt proud to read that the simple shepherds were the first to behold the Holy Family. He could almost feel the golden light of angels as he imagined these pure and humble folk of the field bowing down before the softly cooing Christ Child. What peace he felt. How exquisite it would be to present this otherworldly vision to the loving and simple country folk of his parish.

He had to admit that he was a bit disgruntled by one liberal commentary that claimed shepherds in Israel were afforded no civic respect. It said that shepherds were such notorious thieves and liars that they were excluded from acting as witnesses in all judicial matters. Those who followed the letter of the Jewish laws were forbidden to buy wool or milk from them because it was just assumed that anything a shepherd had to sell must have been stolen.

Pastor Loeson immediately put this less-than-flattering description out of his head. It posed far too great a threat to the romantic picture he had already painted in his head. What's more, some of his own flock raised a few sheep. Surely, they wouldn't take kindly to such a rude depiction of their trade. He was too new to risk offending his members. He brushed the warning aside. That was his first mistake.

Michael had a plan. He would bring the Christmas story right into the lives of these South Dakota farmers by using a visual aid that was close to them. And what would make a better visual aid than a sheep and a shepherd? But somehow that was not enough. He wanted to surprise them. And what would be more surprising than a shepherd and his entire flock of sheep suddenly appearing right there in the sanctuary before them? He started to look for a shepherd and his flock. To be sure that it would be a complete surprise, he told no one of his plan. That was his second mistake.

Now, as the pastor moved from coffee pot to coffee pot, he began to hear stories about an old crusty figure by the name of Jack Jonas. As far as he could figure, Jack was the closest thing the county had to a shepherd. So Pastor Loeson got in his car and headed out into the hills to strike up a deal with Jack Jonas. That was his third mistake.

Jack didn't belong to a church. To hear Jack tell the story, it was difficult for him to get away on Sundays, what with watching the sheep and all. To hear his neighbors tell the story, his Sunday-morning absenteeism had more to do with the trips he made to town on Saturday night than they did with his high level of compassion for his sheep. It only took one look at Jack to know that the truth of the matter was something far different. It was a matter of discomfort: Jack's discomfort sitting in a pew and any respectable church member's discomfort sitting in any pew in Jack's proximity.

Jack lived in what could benevolently be called an RV on the extreme edge of some property he rented from the Wilsons. In the summer, he drove both it and his sheep out into the hills. When the season threatened snow, he parked it right next to a huge pole barn where he wintered his flock. He shared his abode with an assortment of border collies, blue heelers, wool ticks, and sticktight fleas.

Pastor Loeson didn't know why Jack laughed so heartily when he told him about his idea. Unwittingly, he shrugged it off as a kind of Yuletide frivolity. He also didn't notice that Jack was a bit overzealous about the importance of the element of surprise, but you really couldn't blame a young pastor for being so focused on the event that he missed the interpersonal subtext. Jack said he could come up with about a dozen sheep for the Christmas morning extravaganza. He'd wait in the old alleyway about a quarter of a mile down the road from the church. When he saw that everyone was inside, he would pull up to the front door of the church with his cousin's pickup and wait for the preacher's signal from the sacristy window.

On Christmas morning, Michael Loeson waited excitedly for Virginia Rathmeier to finish her solo. When he recognized the end of the piece was near, he slipped into the sacristy and waved at Jack through the window. Then he stepped into the pulpit and began to read the gospel for the day.

"And in that region, there were shepherds out in the field, keeping watch over their flock by night . . ."

With perfect timing, the wooden doors at the back of the church burst open. The whole congregation turned when they heard Jack whistle at his dog, Buster. Buster yipped, and the sheep bunched together, unable to believe that they were really supposed to go into this building. Buster placed a well-aimed nip, and the flock flowed down the center aisle like a woolly flood.

Pastor Loeson beamed at the authenticity of it all. The human flock shifted their disbelieving stares back and forth between the young pastor and the sheep.

Triumphantly, the preacher turned and began to descend from the pulpit, ready to preach the best sermon of his life. But in his regal descent, he failed to notice the electric cord that ran from the pulpit to the Christmas tree. In a futile twist to catch his balance, he knocked over the tree and set off a series of at least five ancient Christmas tree bulb explosions. At the sound of the exploding bulbs, what had been a rather tidy flock of sheep blew up like an agricultural shrapnel bomb. The sheep scattered into the unsuspecting laps of the awestruck congregation.

By the time the pastor got to his feet, a half dozen poinsettias had been knocked from their stands, the baptismal font was upended, and one of the smaller ewes had jumped onto the pastor's chair and was prepared to make a leap of faith onto the altar. Pastor Loeson lunged at the ewe and clumsily lifted her, his arms wrapped around her back, her front legs flailing on either side of his head, and her back legs trying to gain purchase on his hips. He didn't know what frightened ewes were apt to do, but he quickly learned as the frightened ewe did it all over his pure-white alb.

He almost cried when he looked out at the congregation and saw half of them staring at Jack as he cursed his way through the assembly. The other half of them was moving toward the shepherd to either help him or kill him. Meanwhile, Buster went about his business, moving back and forth between the center and side aisles as he herded the sheep back into the narthex.

Jack took the frightened ewe from Michael and deftly swung it over his shoulders. As Michael took off his robe to survey the damage, he heard Marguerite Oland say a bit too loudly, "I guess we can't really blame such an inexperienced pastor for not recognizing the danger of associating with some of the more unsavory members of our community." There was rage in Jack's eyes, but for Michael's sake, he held his tongue. The sheep were driven back into the pickup. Someone slammed the tailgate, and an usher threw a sheep-soiled copy of an old story Bible in with the sheep.

When he got back into the sanctuary, several of the women were busy putting things back into their proper places and picking up what the sheep had left behind. Marguerite Oland came up and began brushing off the pastor's chair and telling him that everything was going to be just fine. After all, how could he have known what kind of man Jack Jonas was? She looked him squarely in the eye and said, "Pastor, there are just some people you're better off not getting involved with. Some people don't have the first idea of what Christmas—or Christianity, for that matter—is all about."

He really did have a pretty good sermon that morning, but it was awfully hard for anyone to listen to it. Occasionally, one of the confirmation students would snicker, and he repeatedly caught Martha Larson looking at the carpet and shaking her head. At the door, everyone was polite enough not to say anything to him about his foolishness. Michael decided that from now on, he would stick to the basics.

On Saturday night, while walking through the church getting things ready for Sunday morning, he noticed that the children's Bible he used as a paperweight for the children's bulletins was missing. By the back pew, he found one of Jack's gloves. He picked it up and remembered the look on Jack's face as he was leaving the church. He decided he'd better make a call.

It was Wednesday before he found his way out to the old RV. Jack was waiting for him, the colorful Bible in his hand. "Found this in the pickup when I was cleaning out the manure. It's a little worse for wear. I don't think you're going to want it anywhere near the church. It's good enough for me though. I found that part about the shepherds in here.

"My grandma took me to Sunday school when I was little. I always wanted to be one of them wise men, but old lady Nelson always told me that I was more the shepherd type. I guess she got that right."

He ushered Michael into the RV, emptied a chair of its contents, and offered him a seat. Michael accepted a cup of coffee but declined the flask with which he offered to top it off. Jack opened the Bible. "You ever read the whole story in here that this guy Luke wrote?" He didn't wait for an answer. "They've got all these emperors and governors running around who knows where, and all these rich folk staying in the inn. But none of them have any idea what's going on. You know who the angels come to? Not the stinking politicians. Not the hoity-toity sleeping warm in the inn. The shepherds. And not counting his parents, do you know who the first people to see Jesus are? The shepherds. And do you know who it is that goes and tells everyone what's going on? The shepherds.

"It's almost like God is saying, 'Listen up, you Pious Pollys and you conniving bureaucrats. I know all about your holy talk and your high-rolling backroom bargains, but I'm still God. This time I'm doing things a little different. I'm using this single pregnant kid and these wild-assed shepherds'—sorry, Pastor—'to get things started. I'm not just sending my kid for the holy, the rich, and the powerful. I'm sending him for everybody. If you got a problem with that, get in line because there are a whole lot of people who're used to being first that aren't going to be too happy about being last.'"

Jack caught himself. He realized he was getting a little carried away. Pastor Loeson just sat there and waited for him to go on.

"I heard what that old goat Marguerite Oland said about me. It ain't the first time she's made it clear what she thinks of my type. I can pretty well guess what the rest of them were thinking. Hell, Pastor, I'm no saint. I've been an expert sinner since before you were born. It's not unusual for me to drink too much and think too little. And if I can make a little extra by playing the rules a little loose, then I'm going to do that. I gotta be honest.

When you came out here asking for my help, I was more than happy to get you into trouble. I really am sorry about that. You seem like a nice enough kid, but after a while, a guy like me gets tired of all those sanctimonious blowhards looking down their snouts at me. Maybe I can't recite all their sweet little Bible verses, and maybe I don't have a church full of deacons and lady's aide members who will vouch for me. But I know how to give a guy an honest break, and that's more than they ever did for me. Besides, if God cared about a bunch of crooked shepherds back then, maybe he still cares about this crooked one today. I tell you what. I'll give you even money that if God were to do it today, you wouldn't see him at some high-rise hotel or shiny new church in the suburbs of Sioux Falls. You know where you'd see him? Down at the Salvation Army or the jail or at some refugee camp where they put all the people they don't want hanging around them. Your church folk don't like me too much, and I know a lot of it is my fault. Wouldn't it be funny if Jesus showed up today looking like some ratty old shepherd like me and they treated him like dirt because he came from the wrong side of the county?

"Don't get me wrong. I know I'm no better than them. I don't like rich and holy people any better than they like poor and rowdy people. They are as much outsiders to me as I am an outsider to them. But if we get used to calling everyone outsiders, one day we are all going to be sitting on the inside, waiting for Jesus to come in and join us, and he's going to be out in some stable somewhere with all the outsiders. If that happens, I don't suppose that all the excuses in the world are going to be enough to coax him in."

Jack got up and poured himself another cup of coffee. He stood there, leaning against the counter, looking out at the fields. Normally, Pastor Loeson didn't like to be preached at.

Most preachers are like that. That's why they're preachers, out of self-defense. But today he didn't mind it. He told Jack he could keep the Bible. He told him he hoped that he would find his way back to the church. There was always room for one more sinner, especially an expert sinner like himself. Jack laughed. And he did come back. Not often, but now and again, especially at Christmas. Once, he even saw Jack sitting at a table with Marguerite Oland while she was negotiating with him on the purchase of one of his border collie pups. Jack looked over at Michael Loeson and winked, and while Marguerite was looking the other way, he topped off her coffee with the flask he pulled from his boot.

Ruby Green: The Body of Christ

December 25, 1986

Immediately after church that Christmas morning in 1985, Mable Trogemann, Martha Larson, and Marguerite Oland all agreed to have coffee together the next day. Now, three ladies taking coffee together the day after Christmas may not sound like big news, but let me tell you, these three ladies gathering together at the same house, at the same time is front-page stuff. Thirty years before, each of them had organized their own Bible study circle, and there was hardly a civil word between them since. Their combat was all but mortal. Let me give you an example.

Their Bible studies met on Sunday, Wednesday, and Friday respectively, and not wanting to call attention to themselves, they simply called them the Sunday, Wednesday, and Friday circles. The Pleasant View pastor prior to Pastor Loeson started a newsletter. He told them that it would be easier for him to print announcements from the circles if each of them would come up with a name.

Mable's group met on Sunday, so they had first crack at naming themselves. Their name was reasonable. Since this was Pleasant View Lutheran and since all the members of their Bible study were genuinely pleasant people, it was only fitting that they name themselves the Pleasant Circle.

Martha took the naming of Mable's circle quite personally. "How dare she call her circle the Pleasant Circle? It makes them sound like they are the church's only circle. What does that make us—the Unpleasant Circle? But I know we can rise above this insult to the Christian women of our circle. I move that we call ourselves the Love Circle. We, at least, will have a name that truly exemplifies the character of our group."

Marguerite didn't even wait for her circle to meet. On the way to her circle meeting, she dropped the new name off at the pastor's office. "It is simple," she said, "but it sends a clear message to the other Bible study groups. Our name shall be the Christian Martys Circle. It's not as flashy as the others, but it truly reflects the calling of our little band of disciples." The pastor said he couldn't agree more.

In spite of their history, the three of them met for coffee. Their plan was simple. Never again would they see their sanctuary desecrated the way they saw it desecrated by Pastor Loeson on his first Christmas morning. Beginning on Thanksgiving of the next year, they would watch his every move, monitor every call to be sure there would be no livestock in that year's Christmas worship. They decided they did not want to be too obvious about their surveillance, so for the sake of cover, they appointed themselves the Yuletide Beautification Committee.

When Thanksgiving arrived, they became tireless about their work. They discovered that, geographically, they were perfect for the assignment. Mable lived just north of the country church, Martha lived due south, and Marguerite lived west, on a hill that she said "overlooks our little piece of paradise."

Every time the pastor called on someone the least bit suspicious, the message buzzed through their telephone lines. Every time someone whose character was even the least bit questionable, one of the ladies showed up at the church with a poinsettia for the sanctuary and checked for visible plans of creaturely planning.

On one occasion, when the pastor called on Butch O'Donnell, the county's foremost beekeeper, Michael swore that he saw all three ladies drive past O'Donnell's in Mable's ancient Nash Rambler. Butch said that was highly unlikely.

The day before Christmas Eve, the Beautification Committee was on red alert. The sanctuary was piling up with poinsettias, and the women declared an around-the-clock ecclesiastical observation. Unknowingly, the pastor kept them on their toes.

In the morning, he called on Frank Olsen. Frank was a farmer married to the parish secretary, and he had a hobby. He raised donkeys, the majority of which he sold to an entrepreneur in Iowa who used them on the donkey basketball circuit.

In the afternoon, Pastor Loeson called on Ruby Green. Anyone in town could tell you about Ruby. As long as anyone could remember, Ruby suffered from some kind of anxiety disorder. Right after high school, Ruby's mother acquired a rare respiratory disease. Somehow, Ruby got the idea that her mother's illness had to do with the rainstorm that drenched the entire community during the outdoor commencement exercise. Ruby spent the rest of her adult life feeling guilty, watching over her ailing mother, and fearing that every breath her mother took would be her last. Male suitors were turned away from the door with a vengeance. Salesmen were given one minute to flee and then were sent packing, dripping wet from the contents of the bucket Ruby kept by the door for just such an occasion. Her mother became Ruby's entire life. She read the newspaper to her. They listened to the radio together. On Sundays, Ruby sang to her from their old Norwegian hymnbook.

When Ruby's mother finally died, Ruby couldn't deal with the silence. She started talking to herself, laughing at her own odd jokes, and arguing both sides of a theological argument at once. She also took to wearing the beautiful lace tablecloth her mother had given her as a graduation gift. It had never graced a table. There had never been any opportunity for guests. Now, in a morbid tribute to her mother, it graced Ruby's own bony frame. She went nowhere without it. To be honest, Ruby became quite creative in the ways she wore the old tablecloth. One day it would appear as a shawl, the next as a sort of elaborate turban, and finally as a kind of backward apron over her bright-blue skirt. She'd tell anyone she met the most intimate details about the tablecloth and the woman who made it for her, so people made a habit of avoiding Ruby.

The pastor did not follow suit. He listened for hours as Ruby talked about her mother. Ruby told him that when she wore the tablecloth, she felt close to her mother. She said that sometimes, late at night, she longed to be held by her mother just one more time. When she wrapped the cloth around her, it was almost as if her mother was wrapping her arms around her. The pastor said he understood. He visited her on a regular basis. On the day before

Christmas Eve, he made one of those calls, and that call made the Terrible Threesome terribly nervous.

That afternoon, an enclosed horse trailer left the Olsen place, and Martha was sure she could smell donkey in there. At sunset, the pastor's car appeared back at the parsonage next to the church, and at seven thirty, the pickup with the horse trailer appeared in front of the church. The Yuletide Beautification Committee sprang into action. They each grabbed their last poinsettia and headed for the sanctuary.

When they got there, the church appeared dark. They entered slowly through the front door, the leaves of their poinsettias trembling. Once they were inside the tiny pitch-black narthex, they could just make out candlelight flickering through the crack between the thick oaken doors that separated them from the sanctuary. Just as they were about to enter, the phone rang, and they could hear the pastor's heavy feet running toward the back of the church. Mable spooked and pulled the other two women inside the doorway that led to the balcony. Just as they got the door closed, they heard the pastor rush past. With silent signals, Mable pointed up the stairs, and the trio began to climb. At the top of the stairs, they stopped as they heard a car door slam outside. Looking through the little windows at the top of the stairs, they saw Ruby Green waving good-bye to her ride and then looking wistfully down at the package she carried.

The women turned their backs on Ruby and crept to the front of the balcony. The shadows from the pew candles danced on the ceiling, and even before they reached the front of the balcony, they could see the white lights on top of the Christmas tree. When they peered over the railing, they gasped at the beauty of what they saw. There in the candlelight were Mary and Joseph and the holy

Christ Child himself. The parents were totally captivated by the cooing child and whispered back and forth as they watched the tiny baby in the manger. In the midst of the Christmas furor, the women had forgotten that—since the first of October—donkeys were not the only things that Frank and Betty were raising. Betty had given birth to their firstborn son, and now the three of them were in the front of the church. Mom and Dad were dressed as Mary and Joseph, and the baby was wearing only Pampers as he lay in the manger. The scene was so beautiful that not even Marguerite could think of a thing to say.

The silence was broken by the slamming of the church door below them. In walked Ruby Green. Ruby's eyes were fixed on the package she carried, but halfway down the aisle, she looked up and stopped dead in her tracks. The sacred scene held her in awe. After a moment, she walked forward and knelt down before the Holy Family. Gently, she touched the child and whispered to the parents. Then, haltingly, she opened the package she carried. Inside, carefully pressed and folded, was the tablecloth her mother had given her. With all the dignity of the magi, she laid the tablecloth on the floor and carefully unfolded it. Ever so gently, Betty placed the baby on the cloth. Ruby, with loving hands, wrapped the babe in the cloth and placed it in the manger. She paused, looked at the baby, and with the slowness of age, bent down and kissed it. With a final loving touch, she stroked the cloth and then left.

The women left the poinsettias in the balcony. Silently, they crept down the stairs, stopping at the bottom to check that the coast was clear.

The next night, they sat together in the same pew. There were tears in their eyes as they watched the Holy Family kneeling there in front of that huge bank of poinsettias. They saw the Christ Child held firmly in the folds of Ruby's tablecloth. On the way out, the three of them took the pastor aside, and you could see him smiling and shaking his head. "Yes, yes, of course," he said. "That is a wonderful idea."

The next morning, the church was beautiful again with all those poinsettias surrounding the altar and the simple white lights illuminating the tree. On the altar, the silver chalice reflected the lights of the tree. The bread was fresh. You could smell its sweet aroma mixed with the soft scent of the pine needles. And there—under the bread and the wine, across the top of that gracious altar, with the beautiful blue of the vestments peeking through it—was the most beautiful lace tablecloth any had ever seen. The three chairs of the circles made sure that it was there every Communion Sunday after that, holding the body of Christ: just the way Ruby Green thought it should.

Matt Larson: The Holy Cows

December 25, 1987

It doesn't matter where you're from; everybody has somebody they call or at least think of as family. And it seems that every one of those families has someone who has appointed himself or herself the family joker. In Matt's family, Great-Uncle Ed was the self-appointed joker; and more often than not, Matt was the jokee.

This particular year, the family was gathered at Uncle Ed's farm on Christmas Eve. Normally, the Larsons gathered on Christmas Day, but Cousin Ruth had moved to Bismarck, North Dakota, and fallen in love with some soldier there. Grandma said that any man who wanted to marry into her family would have to meet with her approval first. The poor boy had to be back on Christmas Day, so the family moved their Christmas celebration to Christmas Eve.

Matt did not like this arrangement. Being at Uncle Ed's house on Christmas Eve meant missing his own Christmas program and going to some little country church program instead. He was especially disappointed because this year, his church in Sioux Falls was doing *The Cosmic Christmas Spectacular,* and he was a pretty sure bet to land the disc jockey role in the "Christmas 2020" scene. Now he had to attend some Podunk church; watch some hick farm kids dress up like shepherds, angels, and wise men; and sing old-fashioned Christmas carols. It was enough to make him puke.

Uncle Ed met Matt and his family at the door. Matt's folks went in first, and Matt moped behind. After Matt came in, Uncle Ed stuck his head out the door and pretended to squint down the road. "Well, where is she?"

"Where's who?" Matt pouted.

"Well, your fiancée! Who'd you think? Ruthie brought hers. I was just sure you'd bring one too. Did you make her wait in the car?" Uncle Ed kidded.

"Get real, Uncle Ed," Matt grumbled.

"Well, it's probably better that you didn't anyway. Your grandma's got Ruthie's beau so nervous, he's spent most of the day in the bathroom anyway. I'd better go check and see if we got any toilet paper left."

Matt laughed but Aunt Gladys shouted, "Ed, shut the door and leave that poor boy alone."

Ed winked and put his finger to his lips. "Shush now," he whispered. "Don't tell your aunt what I said. You know she's kinda sensitive about these things." He put his hands on Matt's shoulders and followed him into the kitchen.

Matt made it through the big Christmas supper, managing to laugh at not a single of Uncle Ed's jokes. He wanted to make it clear to everyone that he was not where he wanted to be. After the meal, Uncle Ed leaned back in his chair and hooked his big thumbs through his suspenders. He drummed his fingers on his chest while he spoke. Matt was finishing his milk.

"You know why that milk's so sweet, don't ya, Matt?"

Matt ignored him.

"It's 'cause we've got religious cows. Ain't that right, Gladys?"

Gladys said nothing, but her eyes twinkled.

Uncle Ed continued. "Yup, they're religious, all right. They pray and worship just like you and me." He paused and looked down at his shoe, playing Matt like a fish. "Yup, ya see it was the cows that were the first to see the Lord. You remember he was born in a stable, don't ya? Well, when Mary gave birth, the cows were looking right over Joseph's shoulder, and when they saw the newborn baby, they started to cry big old cow-sized tears. They fell right down on their bovine knees and worshipped Jesus. Ever since then, the offspring of those blessed cattle followed the lead of their ancestors. Every Christmas Eve, right at the stroke of midnight, they fall down on their knees and worship the Lord. I've been in the stable hundreds of times myself and seen them do it."

Matt looked at Uncle Ed through squinting eyes, but Ed didn't return his look. He just stuck his hand in his pocket and pulled out his pocket watch. "Speaking of worship, we'd better get going or none of us is going to get a seat."

They all piled into their cars and headed for Pleasant View. Inside the church, they squeezed into pews and waited for worship to begin. Matt sat with his hands deep in his pockets and looked at his shoes as he swung them beneath the pew, trying to look as bored as a kid dared to look on Christmas Eve. He sang halfheartedly, catching himself when too much enthusiasm crept into his voice. He tried to be unimpressed, but the candles, the soft lights, and the scent of pine slowly worked their magic.

His eyes were riveted to the front of the church as a young couple wrapped their little baby in what seemed to be a lace tablecloth and laid him in an old wooden manger. Behind Mary and Joseph stood one of the Sunday school children, holding a life-sized cardboard cow. The child's face beamed through the hole cut where the cow's face should have been.

Matt sneaked a peek at his uncle. Uncle Ed was enwrapped in the scene. Beyond Uncle Ed, Matt saw the candlelight dance on the brass of the young soldier's uniform. Matt looked back at Uncle Ed, and this time, Uncle Ed returned the look. He motioned at the cow with his thumb, winked at Matt, and silently mouthed "religious cows." Matt rolled his eyes and pretended to read his bulletin. One of the high school girls sang "Silent Night" and the service was over.

He was quiet on the way back to Uncle Ed's as his parents tried to figure out who each of the children belonged to. "No, don't you remember? Henrietta was a Nelson. She married the Olson boy whose dad got his arm caught in the power take-off. They had those eight kids. The granddaughter's mom was one of the twins. You know, the one that you could tell wasn't the other one because she had the birthmark right in the middle of her left earlobe. Only thing that kept 'em from being identical. That and her temper."

Matt watched the digital clock on the dashboard click past 11:49 p.m. In the midst of all the cars unloading in front of the farmhouse, he slipped away from the crowd and headed for the barn.

Uncle Ed had long since retired from farming full-time. What few cows he had left had long since stopped giving milk and lived in a lean-to stable attached to the east side of the barn. His cattle were more like children than livestock, living in the luxury of new straw every day and the warm flow of Uncle Ed's chatter.

Matt reached the stable and fumbled with the latch on the door. The barn boards rattled in the struggle. When the door finally opened, Matt gasped at what he saw. There in the moonlight, two of the three cows appeared to be getting up off their prayerful knees. Their old, bony hips were high in the air as their weight rested on their front legs folded beneath them. They grunted as they swayed to straighten one front leg and then the other, rising from their awkward prayerful position to their feet. The third cow lay on the straw, lazily chewing her cud. Matt circled the room with his eyes, thinking that somewhere, Uncle Ed must be hiding and orchestrating the whole affair with hidden ropes. But there were no ropes, no Uncle Ed.

He stepped inside and slowly closed the door behind him. He put his hand on the rough wall and felt his way through the near darkness. Halfway across the room, he stumbled over Uncle Ed's one-legged stool and yelped as he struck his shin on a milk can. Holding his knee to his chest, he did a one-legged dance, squinting his eyes and whispering "Ouch, ouch, ouch!"

He stopped his dance short as the third cow began to roll its legs under it. Gracefully, she raised her rear end up in the air and stood for a moment with her rear in the air and her weight resting on her front knees. For that split second, she looked for all the world like she was praying. Then, gathering her strength, she rocked off one knee and then another and came to a full standing position.

"Religious cows, huh, Uncle Ed? Nice try. They just look like they're praying when they're trying to stand up."

Matt walked past the cows and sat on the long feedbox that ran the length of the stable. He sat there a long time. One by one, the cows lay back down, and the room became silent except for the rhythm of their breathing. Matt sat on the manger, peacefully watching them. The bright straw glistened in the moonlight that flooded in through the four panes of the eastern window. Through the window, Matt could see the deep midnight sky with its bright pinpoints of light. Icy clouds floated across the moon. The breathing of the cows and the warmth of the room lulled him into a trance as he watched the little flakes of snow drift off the roof, across the window, and out of sight. He could smell the rich mix of manure, fresh straw, dusty oats, old wood and warm cows.

There in that cozy place, the magic of Christmas spun its spell. For a moment—just for a moment—Matt was no longer sitting in an old barn at Uncle Ed's farm. The sky didn't belong to South Dakota. The stars weren't shining on down on Pleasant View. He was in a stable behind an inn, looking out at a bright Judean sky, with stars shining down on the little town of Bethlehem. For a moment, just a moment, Matt was surrounded by the most holy of cows—warm, breathing, chewing, watching, holy cows. These cows were holy not because they knelt or prayed but because they were chosen to be in the presence of the holy Christ Child. And as they lay there, breathing the holy air and chewing their holy cud, the miracle of God being with us happened.

With the cry of a tiny baby laid on the bright yellow straw, the room was no longer just a stable. It was a sanctuary—a holy of holies holding the very presence of God. The hills and trees and grass that surrounded this old barn were no longer just countryside. The countryside became the center of the universe, the throne room of the king. The world was no longer just the world. It was the holy dwelling place of God. And every young woman, every old man, every child, every person on the face of the earth was no longer just a person. They were witnesses to the miracle of the incarnation. Matt who was no longer some kid, the butt of Uncle Ed's jokes. He was Matthew, the chosen of the Lord. Matt didn't have the words to say it, but he felt the truth of it. Because of that holy night, he and every inhabitant of the planet Earth had started down the long road of redemption. The presence of God among common cows, common folks, on common soil was transforming. On this holy night, it didn't matter if you were in Sioux Falls or in Bethlehem or Timbuktu. There was only one thing to do: bow down in holy worship.

Matt knelt in the straw.

He looked out at the sky, at the icy clouds hanging on the moon. Suddenly, they were no longer clouds. They were an angelic host singing. Not like the children at Pleasant View, but like the whole state of South Dakota—farmers and construction workers, bankers and doctors, and lawyers and musicians. Old people, young people, all singing in perfect pitch, full-throated, a song so rich and wide and sweet that the walls of the stable shook, and the shepherds down below trembled and hid their heads. "Glo-o-o-o-o-o-o-o-o-o-o-o-ria in Excelsis Deo." This was the truly cosmic Christmas, not wrapped in tinny amplified music but in the music of the planets and the stars.

As Matt sat there, it was almost as if he could hear the shepherds coming toward the stable. He could hear the crunching

23

of their footsteps in the snow. He heard the stable door rattle as they tried to open it. Matt held his breath. The cow farthest from him rolled onto her legs and began to raise her hindquarters. The second cow followed suit. For a long instant, they held their position on their knees.

He looked at the door. Was he dreaming, or was it opening? Someone gasped and then whispered, "What the . . . ?" Matt squatted to look under the cows that had made it to their feet. There, he saw a pair of dress uniform blue slacks and spit-polished boots.

His uncle called from the house, "Is he in there?"

Matt stood up, and the soldier gave a little jump, voicing a somewhat less-than-heavenly exaltation. Matt waved sheepishly. "Yah, he's in here," the soldier yelled back. They walked together back to the house. Uncle Ed waited for them at the door.

"Well, we found ya." Then he whispered, "By the way, did either of you boys see my religious cows kneeling out there?"

The soldier looked at Matt and stuck his hands in his pockets. Matt motioned Uncle Ed closer and whispered, "We saw 'em all right, Uncle Ed. But they weren't religious cows. They're holy cows."

Uncle Ed got a puzzled look on his face and squinted at Matt. Then he straightened up and laughed from his belly. "Heh heh, that's a better one yet. I've got the original holy cows. Wait till I tell Gladys this one." He led the two into the house. "Lookee what I found, Gladys. A couple of shepherds out watching their holy cows by night."

Magda the Magnificent:
The Light of the World

December 25, 1988

There is not a person alive who can remember a time when Magda was not a member of Pleasant View Lutheran Church. She is as much a part of Pleasant View as the creaking hardwood floor or the towering old oak pulpit.

Now, don't misunderstand me. To say that Magda is such a vital part of Pleasant View is not to say that her name is the first name that comes to mind when someone mentions the name *Pleasant View Lutheran Church*. Magda is not like Marguerite Oland. There is a rumor that Marguerite wandered out onto the prairie one December afternoon, stomped her foot, pointed her finger at the ground, and refused to move until they came and built the church around her. Actually, Marguerite has only been around those parts for fifty years or so. She just has a way of reading herself into Pleasant View's history. She spoke as if she certainly would have been there to found the church if God hadn't had her someplace else, taking care of something a whole lot more important.

Magda was a different kind of woman. No, she wasn't there when the church was founded. The church was a whole lot older than either Magda or Marguerite. But Magda was born just across the section from the church. There were no fences between her father's farm and the graveyard. Long before Magda could walk, her father and mother carried her to the font in their little church, and Magda had worshiped there every Sunday since. In her eighty-four years, she could only remember missing services once, and that was way back when she was sixteen. Except for that one sad Sunday, Magda was always there. Always willing. Never saying much and never making a show of things. She never chaired anything but always helped. People may not remember to mention her name when someone asked, "Who was at the meeting the other night?" but more than likely she was there. If you looked, you would see her sitting back in one of the corners, raising her hand when they asked who would bring cookies or do the dishes or help with the church cleaning. Magda was a presence, warm and smiling, hands folded in her broad lap and head tilted just enough to let you know she was listening. She was quick to thank you, too embarrassed to correct you—a safe place to be when it seemed like everyone else was out to get you.

That's why Pastor Loeson found his way to her house. He didn't know it, but he was looking for a safe place to hide, and the picture of Magda's house jumped right into his mind. That's why he turned the corner to pull into her yard rather than drive on down the section to the church.

Pastor Loeson was getting ready for the Christmas Eve service. He had chosen all the parts for the worship except for the part of the Christmas angel. It wasn't a speaking part, but it was an important part. The Christmas angel walked down the aisle, carrying a candle, right in the middle of the worship service. Mary, Joseph, and the baby were already in their place in the front, the shepherds were crouched all around them, and one of the children began to gently ring the finger cymbals.

In the back of the church, the dark wooden doors opened, and there stood the Christmas angel, dressed in white with gold garland in her hair, illumined by the light of a single candle she carried down the aisle as the wise men followed regally behind. The angel walked to the front of the church, found her way through the shepherds, and stepped up on a little platform behind the Holy Family, casting her light on the precious scene.

The shrinking ranks of children had been all used up as shepherds, sheep, and wise men. The Holy Family was a real family of mother, husband, and the newest member of the Pleasant View congregation. That left only the part of the Christmas angel, and Marguerite Oland decided she was perfect for the part.

Pastor Loeson had nothing against Marguerite. She was a pillar of the church. She was perhaps the most visible worker within the congregation. He even understood that she had something to do with starting the church, but he was unclear as to the details. But Pastor Loeson also knew Marguerite's weaknesses. He knew that putting her, the congregation's self-proclaimed historic orator, in front of the church with every eye riveted to her and every ear keenly attuned to her, was a temptation greater than Marguerite could withstand. What was intended to be a silent angel, beautiful and still, would suddenly be changed into a kind of spiritual

Barbara Walters, expounding on the importance of the scene that was taking place before her. Pastor Loeson slammed the door of his car, trying to free himself of such an unseemly picture. There was a dangerous trap being laid for him, and he wasn't ready to face it yet. Not when he could escape into Magda's warm kitchen and soft molasses cookies.

Halfway through his third cup of coffee, Pastor Loeson found a way out of the trap. His eyes fell on an old red kerosene lantern sitting on top of a preserves cabinet by the porch door. It looked well used, and the box of matches sitting next to it suggested that it still worked. He asked Magda where it came from. She said it had been her grandfather's, but he gave it to her when she was just sixteen. She said she had come to a point where she couldn't do chores without it (which was kind of silly, what with electricity in all the buildings). She didn't need the lantern, but she had used it for so many years, she just couldn't leave the kitchen without it. It had been her companion, she told him, hanging in the henhouse as she picked the eggs, swinging to and fro as she walked through the alleyway to get their feed in the early morning. She told how once, when her husband was still alive, she held the lantern at the end of each potato row late on Good Friday evening as she and her husband tried to get the last of the planting done.

Pastor Loeson told her he wanted to use the lantern on Christmas Eve, and he wanted her to carry it. She laughed at first because she thought he was kidding. Then she pleaded with him to find someone else. But he said his mind was made up. She would be the Christmas angel. She said Christmas angels shouldn't be eighty-four years old. He said angels never age.

She blushed and said, "All right."

When Christmas Eve finally came, the church was packed. With homespun pomp, the living menagerie of Christmas characters found their way down the aisle to the front of the church. While they waited, shepherds fidgeted with their bathrobes and the sheep kept moving their elastic ears back to the center of their heads. Mary and Joseph laid their baby, wrapped in a lace tablecloth, in the manger. The church grew quiet as little Marcie Quam rung the finger cymbals, and Magda began her walk down the aisle.

The pastor was right. In the lantern's light, she looked ageless. The light danced between the gold of her garland and the silver of her hair. Her face seemed to radiate as much warm light as the old luminary she carried. To be sure, she swayed when she walked, ambling slowly to protect aging hips. Her ascent to the top of the low platform was slow but magnificent, and when she reached her place, she raised the lantern with a practiced elegance that only years of familiarity could bring.

There was silence. And then, softly, the organ began to play "Silent Night." Magda looked into the lantern to avoid the eyes of the crowd. As she watched the flame glow within, she was transported to another year, another day, sixty-eight years ago, the day she received the lantern.

She was sixteen. She was the oldest child of her mother and a reluctant father who, one evening, went out to check on the buildings in the north forty and never came back. There was so great of a space between her and the next child that she quite naturally became a surrogate mother as her own mother was forced to play the role of father.

Her grandfather also lived in the farmhouse with them. He was a wonderful man with pure-white hair and a long drooping mustache. He had long since set himself free form the bounds of reality and had taken to talking with people who weren't there. He went with Magda as she gathered the eggs, carrying the prized lantern that was one of his first purchases in the new country to which he had immigrated. As he stood with an unsteady hand holding the light, he addressed one or two of his ghostly companions as they stood by his side. On other occasions, he sat in the rocking chair and held a skein of yarn, mumbling as Magda wrapped the woolen cord into a ball for her mother.

Things went well until his conversations with his imaginary friends took on an argumentative quality. At first it was funny when he stood up at the dinner table and yelled, "Schmitty, you don't know what the hell you're talking about!" Or when he spun around, pointing an accusatory finger and threatening, "Siggurd, I'll thank you very much to keep your damn mouth shut if you can't keep from interrupting me all the time!" But as time went by, Grandpa became more and more violent.

It all came to a head early one Sunday morning, when the entire household was awakened by a shotgun blast. Magda and her mother rushed into the kitchen to find Grandpa stark naked, screaming out of the hole he had just blasted through the porch door. "And don't ever come back," he thundered as the lantern flickered on the kitchen table. He laid the shotgun across the arms of the rocker, sat down at the kitchen table, and started to cry. Magda laid a dish towel across his lap and held his hand, too afraid to say a word; too much Magda to let go. She looked into the familiar light of the lantern to steady herself.

When her mother finally got him up and dressed, he followed her to the door like a child. At the door, he stopped and walked back to the kitchen table. He picked up the lantern and handed it to

Magda. "That's my girl," he said. "You always were the light of my life. Keep the lantern filled for me. It's yours to take care of now."

And for a moment, he held her cheek in his hand, looked into her eyes with a look of understanding that held Magda for the rest of her life. With that, he turned and rode away to the county home with Magda's mother. Magda sat at the table and cried until she fell asleep, the old lantern burning securely beside her. When she woke up, she put out the lantern, filled it with kerosene, and set it back up on the preserves cabinet.

Pastor Loeson broke into Magda's dream as he stared to read the Gospel from John. "In him was life, and the life was the light of all. The light shines in the darkness and the darkness has not overcome it."

She lowered the lantern, and the pastor began to speak of the lights in his life. He told of a Savior born to send light into the world where there was entirely too much darkness. He talked about his mother. He talked about a friend who held him through a night of terror. And then he talked about Magda, holding the lantern, bringing light into this dark room. "If only we all took the opportunity to be a light to others."

The congregation looked at Magda, Magda the Magnificent. They thought about her ever-present light and they smiled. When the service was over, Magda rushed to grab a coffeepot so she could look busy and no one would talk to her about her part in the play. The people were kind. They touched her shoulder, told her she looked beautiful, and asked her where she got the lantern. She said she was just keeping it burning for a friend and excused herself to go and fill the pot. The pastor winked at her and Magda blushed. At eighty-four, she was too busy shining to pay too much attention to compliments.

Frederica Olson: The Magnificat

December 25, 1989

It was a lean year at Pleasant View Lutheran Church. The drought made the harvest scant. Visitors vacationed elsewhere, and not a single baby was born. The high school class dwindled to five: four boys and Frederica Olson, a sadly named teenage girl who never showed up for anything.

Pastor Loeson stewed over the Christmas program. There was no child young enough to pass for even a divinely born infant. Most of the young couples were too busy watching their toddlers to pose as Mary and Joseph. The others were newly married and too shy to pose as parents of a newborn.

He turned to the high school students for help. In an uncharacteristic fit of pre-Christmas tomfoolery, the students met during Sunday school and selected the Holy Family. Jesus was to be played by Ned Johnson's Raggedy Andy doll, whom they stage named Baby Doe. Joseph would be played by their own Spike

Nelson. Spike was formerly known as Mark Nelson but that was before he discovered styling mousse and the word *bogus*.

Mary was to be no one else than Frederica Olson.

They wrote down their list of characters and giggled as they waited for the explosion that would occur when they handed it to Pastor Loeson. But Pastor Loeson did not return. Finally, just as Mrs. Oland was ringing the bell to end Sunday school, the pastor rushed in and grabbed the list. To their dismay, without reading it, he folded it and stuffed it into his Bible.

This put a whole new light on things. They never considered that their list might actually be used. In a sheer fit of fright, Spike promised he'd wash his hair and don appropriate headgear. Ned Johnson promised he'd come up with another Baby Jesus. As a class, they drafted a letter to Frederica. In a final spurt of desperation, they signed the pastor's name, hoping that calling on a higher authority would somehow move Frederica to show up and save their collective hides.

No one ever told Frederica that she was beautiful. Not her mother. Not the boys in her class. And certainly not her father. But it really didn't matter. After sixteen years of being Art Olson's girl, she wouldn't have believed it anyway.

Art Olson was as mean as any father in Pleasant View could be. His father had raised him to be mean, and he had never encountered any good reason to abandon his education. He was the one who insisted that his daughter be named after his grandmother. His wife pleaded with him. Yes, it was a beautiful name, but what kid wouldn't laugh at a name like *Frederica*? But Art Olson was not a man to change his mind. He was mean. It was only a graceful irony of life that kept him from living out his cruelty to the full extent of his desire.

Four years ago, Art decided that his wife was cheating on him. The fact was that Art's wife wasn't cheating on him, but Art never allowed the facts to cloud his decision-making process. After he decided she was guilty, nothing else mattered. He went screaming around town in his pickup, creating sordid tales of her indiscretion. He bellowed them out to anyone who had the misfortune of coming within earshot of his beer-soaked voice.

After he finished his third six-pack of righteousness, he went home to teach her a lesson. She was in the basement washing out his work clothes when he came raging into the house. He heard her slam the door on the dryer, ran to the cellar door, and kicked it open. When she had the nerve to back away from him, he started down the stairs after her, but his legs got all tangled up, and he fell headlong down the steps.

There was a note for Frederica when she got home from school. She felt sick when she read it and rode her bike to the hospital. She visited him every day in the hospital, but this time, not even his meanness could make him better. When he came home from the hospital, he had a steel plate in his head. He couldn't walk. He couldn't think. He could only lie in bed and be angry while the ones he was angry at waited on him.

After a year, his savings and insurance were all used up, and Frederica's mom had to go to work. She got a job on the evening shift at the powdered-egg plant in the next county. Every day, she picked up Frederica at school and rushed her home before she headed out for eight hours of cracking eggs into a vat.

Frederica spent the next three years as a prisoner to her father's needs. He'd scream out what he wanted, and she'd run to get it. When she would arrive at his bedside, he would tell her how slow or how stupid or how ugly she was, and she would just walk away, determined that next time she'd be smarter or faster or prettier.

When she got the letter from Pastor Loeson, she knew immediately that it was not from Pastor Loeson. (She was certain that he knew how to spell *Lutheran*.) But her mom called Betty Olson, the secretary, and she said that Frederica's name was on the rough draft of the bulletin she had received from Pastor Loeson. She said they had a costume for her, and she was supposed to memorize the Magnificat, Luke 2:46-55. Yes, it was all right if she couldn't make it to rehearsal. All she had to do was say her line and walk with Joseph to the manger. One of the boys was bringing a baby Jesus for her. There was no mistake. Frederica had been chosen.

For the next week, Frederica did not turn on the TV once. Between her father's demands and harassments, she paced the living room, memorizing her piece. She said it over and over again. Changing the emphasis from one word to the next. Gesturing with her hand for dramatic flair. She tried speaking it with an English accent like the women on public television, and then she tried whispering it passionately, imitating the chiffon voices of the women who prayed for money on the *Power of Praise* show.

All the time she practiced, she felt a strange feeling that moved back and forth between the pit of her stomach and the center of her heart. It swung between terror and pride, honor and humiliation. She had never been chosen before. In an awkward sort of way, it changed things for her. On Friday, she walked past her father's room, speaking her part. Her concentration was so great that she never noticed that he was awake and watching her. His voice startled her.

"Jesus Christ, who the hell do you think you are anyway, dancing around here like the Queen of Sheba? You're so stupid you've even started talking to yourself." At that moment, she was absorbed in her role as Mary, and before her head could edit the response, her heart answered. "How dare you talk to me that way? You're so ignorant you don't even know who I am or what I've been called to do."

She gasped at what she had said. She tensed, ready for his attack, but he just looked at her—like he was seeing her for the first time, like he was trying to figure out if maybe she really was someone important. He was too confused to attack. For the first time ever, he was the one who looked away first. She walked away from his room, and she felt that funny feeling growing inside again.

On Christmas Eve, the church was packed like it always was. Frederica's aunt arrived late to watch her brother, and Frederica got to the church at the last possible moment. Betty rushed Frederica off to the ladies' room so she could get dressed, and her mom found a seat.

Frederica and Betty stood before the mirror in the ladies' room. Betty stood behind her and brushed Frederica's long brown hair and then pinned the soft muslin shawl on her, letting it fall over her shoulders and down her back. Frederica closed her eyes and tried to remember her lines.

Betty stepped to the side and looked into the mirror. She gasped, "My goodness, girl. Look at yourself. If you don't look like the Virgin Mary, I don't know who does. Look how beautiful you are."

Just then Mrs. Oland called, and Betty rushed from the room.

Frederica looked into the mirror. This time the words she whispered were not Mary's but her own:

> My heart praises the Lord;
> My soul is glad because of God my Savior,
> for he has remembered me, his lowly servant.

In spite of his promise, Mark Nelson showed up with his hair spiked. But even with that, once he was robed, he made a handsome Joseph. Ned Johnson talked his older sister into coming home for Christmas a day early and lending her baby girl to the congregation for the Nativity scene.

Frederica stepped into the spotlight and spoke her lines perfectly. Gallantly, Joseph led her to the manger, and Ned's sister slipped silently onto the stage and eased the baby into her arms. Frederica gently cradled the infant in her arms and swayed back and forth as the seventh-grade girls sang "Silent Night."

For a moment, her fear melted and the glow on her face expressed the strange feeling that had taken up residence in her heart. Her mother cried, and Frederica basked in the wonder of being chosen.

Only the angels knew how blessed was the earth to receive such a child—a child who would strangely change the order of things in the lives of the earth's broken people. Only the angels and Mary knew how different the world would be because of that night's birth. But like Mary, Frederica was beginning to understand. She felt as though a birth had taken place inside of her, like a tiny portrait had been etched upon her heart, a vision of a child chosen by God. To be sure, it was an elusive etching, one that mean men and thoughtless children could obscure. But one that could not be wiped out. One that, for a moment, Frederica could see clearly. She was a child of God chosen by God's own hand, exalted by God's own love.

When the service was over, the crowd moved downstairs. Frederica's mother found Frederica and kissed her. She whispered in her ear, "I had forgotten how beautiful you really are. I'm so proud of you." They talked and giggled like two schoolgirls. When the four boys from Frederica's class moved over to talk to Frederica, her mother politely disappeared into the crowd.

"You did a nice job," Spike said. "We're really glad you were Mary." Ned blurted out, "Yeah, you don't know how glad we are you showed up," Spike gave him a sharp elbow in the ribs.

"I think I do know how glad you guys are," Frederica said. Then she leaned forward and whispered, "Lutheran is spelled L-U-T-H-E-R-A-N." The four boys blushed. Frederica laughed the kind of laugh that the boys thought they could get used to hearing. The Pleasant View Lutheran Church class of 1993 moved toward the punch bowl with a newfound confidence.

Anton Anderson: The Gift

December 25, 1990

I n the sixth year of his ministry, Pastor Loeson was beginning to get into the rhythm of things. By Thanksgiving, he had all the parts for the Christmas program filled. By December 20, he found the family for the Living Nativity. Not that it was a difficult task. There were only two families in the entire congregation with infants, and one of them was traveling to Sioux Falls for Christmas. So the Lunds were elected. Ginny wasn't exactly the Virgin Mary type, but her daughter Chelsea would make a perfect Jesus and Tom—well, Tom had a beard.

On December 24, Pastor Loeson needed to make just one phone call and everything would be ready. He had to ask Anton Anderson to help distribute the Christmas sacks. Anton wasn't answering his phone, so Michael took a deep breath and descended into the Christian Martyrs Circle Christmas Tea in the fellowship hill.

Anton wasn't answering his phone because he wasn't at home. He was sitting alone in a high-backed mahogany booth in the back room of the Bungalow Café. He sipped his lukewarm coffee and rearranged the little Nativity scene on the table one more time. Orvis, the owner of the Bungalow, put Christmas decorations out to encourage his clientele to try the Magi Meatloaf with Nativity Noodles. Its characters were little wax figurine candles. Thus far, the marketing technique fell short of success. Some vandal actually lit the candles, and as a result, the shepherd was headless and the donkey was swaybacked.

From his hiding place, Anton could hear the music from the radio on the counter out front. In the sunlight of the front room, he could see the line of bright-orange vinyl booths and the sign that Orvis hung in the window in 1968. "Come in and check out our new look!"

He wanted some hot coffee, but he knew that Orvis already thought he was overstaying his welcome. Orvis was a strict man. He was not about to encourage loitering by filling anyone's cup more than twice. Anton sure as hell was not going to be the first man on earth to ask Orvis for a third refill. He knew his limits.

The back room had no windows. Beyond the old pool table with its low-hanging Grain Belt Beer light, a stainless steel cart for the Friday Night Bullhead Feed shared the space with a couple of card tables and a dozen folding chairs. From eight to ten every morning, the card tables were packed with Anton's friends, a dozen coffee-drinking, whist-playing retired farmers. At ten o'clock, they either met their wives out front for coffee or headed over to the co-op where the coffee was bad but free.

It was ten thirty. Anton's wife was at the church with her circle, and Anton didn't go to the co-op anymore. "It's just not the same place anymore," he said. "Used to be a guy could go in there, do some trading, and find out what's going on. Maybe look though some old issues of the *Wallace Farmer*. Now it seems all you get down there is a pack of young pups telling you that everything you did for the last fifty years was all wrong. They come in there, bragging about their artificial insemination and their no-till farming. Now that they got the plows and the bulls idle, I suppose the next thing they'll be wanting is to farm without dirt. Not a one of them knows the first thing about an honest day's work."

Anton's buddies didn't argue with Anton. They just dealt the cards. But they all knew it wasn't the co-op that was changing. It was Anton. Since he stopped milking last May, Anton argued with everybody. Marvin Flatbush said Anton had "retired milker's syndrome." Marvin said, "The reason he used to be so friendly was on account of him being so tired. He spent so much time in the barn he didn't have any energy left for arguing. He was so worn out even a wet tail in the face didn't bother him. When he quit milking last May, he had a whole lifetime of arguing stored up. Now he's so cantankerous that even Orvis's meatloaf is a better companion for lunch."

Anton was famous for his milking. Most of the ranchers raised cattle, but only a handful of them milked. Anton was the most respected of them all. He started milking when he was five and milked without interruption for sixty years. Except for his knee replacement, he never missed a milking. He was in the barn at four thirty every morning and usually didn't get out till after seven. It was the same way at night. He was a driven man. His barn was spotless, and his record book was perfect. They never turned away even a pound of his milk.

And he wasn't like some young guys either. He never missed a church service. Unfortunately, he never heard a sermon either. After getting up at four o'clock and running around in the cold, it was impossible for him to stay awake in a warm pew. But he figured it all evened out. After all, it wasn't easy to master the look of pious reflection while you slept through the sermon. He'd only been caught once. It was in 1963, when old Pastor Jacobson was still there. At the conclusion of every sermon, the pastor said "amen" and the entire congregation stood up to receive a blessing. It was a tricky bit of business, but Anton trained his ear to hear "amen" so that he could stand up on cue the instant he heard it. The day Anton got caught, Pastor Jacobson was preaching on Revelation. In the middle of his sermon, he quoted the heavenly host and cried out "amen." Right there, in the middle of the sermon, in a conditioned response, Anton stood up. He waited for the rest of the congregation to join him. The preacher stopped preaching. Anton nervously looked around and then leaned down to his wife and, in an overly loud whisper, said, "I gotta go to the bathroom." Through some miracle of discipline, Pastor Jacobson and the congregation managed not to laugh. To this day, Anton refuses to admit he sleeps in church.

There was more to Anton's milking than most suspected. Like I said, he was a driven man. The doctor told him he worked too hard. His back took on the permanent shape of a question mark. One knee was replaced and the other needed it. His hip needed it too, but he was too young. For two years, the doctor harped at Anton to quit milking, but Anton wouldn't listen. When he finally took a fall in the feedlot, his wife wouldn't let him in the house until he promised to sell the cows and quit milking. It took Anton a year to make good on his promise. The day after the herd was gone, Anton began his descent into retired milker's syndrome.

So Anton sat alone in the back, waiting for the lunch shift to come in. He moved the little stable in front of him and picked up the Holstein cow with AMPI stamped on its underside. As he looked at the empty stable, he began to feel afraid, like he was about to be caught.

He remembered a cold December evening when he was in junior high. He was supposed to be watching for the milk truck. His dad, Ivor, found him sleeping in the milk room. "Well, I guess now I know what kind of man you're gonna grow up to be: scratching your ass and living off the county. Go on in the house with your mother. I'll wait for the truck. I should have known not to count on you."

Anton could still feel the ache of it in his chest. He spent every day since then trying to prove his father wrong. Ivor never noticed, and now he was in the grave, but that didn't matter. Anton didn't need his dad to serve up the harsh words anymore. He could do it all by himself. Seeing the cow reminded him that it was time for another serving. He gave himself the same lecture he'd been giving himself since May.

"What kind of man is still sitting around the coffee shop at ten thirty in the morning? What kind of man lets a little pain in his knee make him stop earning his keep? Well, Ivor, is this pathetic enough for you? When a cow goes down, at least they can make hamburger out of her. They can't even do that with me. I'm about as productive as that baby in the manger. It won't be long, and they'll be changing my pants too."

He set the lone Holstein on the table with disgust and dug in his pockets for change. He tossed two quarters on the table and swore at the pain in his knee as he stood up. He wasn't all the way straightened up when Ginny "Soon-to-Be-the-Virgin-Mary" Lund rushed in. She looked relieved when she recognized Anton.

"If I don't get in that lady's room this instant, I'm gonna bust," she said. "You watch Chelsea for me." With that, she handed Anton an infant seat stuffed full with a two-month-old baby. Anton tried to argue, but Ginny was gone.

Anton had delivered hundreds of calves in his lifetime, but he could count on the calloused fingers of one hand the number of times he had held a baby. He set the infant seat down on the table like he was depositing a five-gallon bucket. He stuck his hands in his pockets and nervously looked over his shoulder for Ginny to come back. He reached out and touched the car seat, pretending to study its construction, and then he stole a look at the baby.

Her tiny fingers were beautiful—long and slender with perfectly shaped fingernails. Her delicate little nose looked like it had been carved out of Ivory soap, and her precious rose-colored lips looked like they had been painted on in a porcelain doll factory. Her eyes were bright and eager, and it almost looked like she was studying him with her long, intent gaze. She smiled, and Anton moved his hand down to touch her silky hair. She cooed, swung her arms and, with the accidental grace only an infant can muster, grabbed his finger and soon was clinging to it with two warm baby hands.

"You're a beauty, you are," Anton cooed back at the baby. "I bet your momma is proud of you. They don't make china dolls any prettier. What a gift. Your daddy would have to be crazy not to love a little one like you. I bet he wouldn't trade a wagon full of diamonds for you."

"She's Jesus, you know." Ginny's voice made Anton quickly pull his hand free from the baby's grasp. Ginny stepped to his side and picked up the infant seat.

"What?"

"Tonight at the Christmas program, Chelsea's gonna be Jesus. And Pastor said he wanted you to help with the Christmas sacks. I gotta go. Thanks for watching Chelsea. I already wet one pair of pants today. We'll see you tonight."

Anton would have given anything not to go to the program, but his wife said if they didn't go, everybody would talk about it. Anton got the message and went to the service. With all the cars, it seemed like he had to walk half a mile to get to the front door.

Inside, the program had started. The pastor was standing in the back and asked Anton about handing out the sacks. He told him to go through the basement and get the sacks out of the sacristy. Elsie went in and sat on a folding chair in the aisle.

Anton found his way through the basement and up the back stairs into the sacristy. The room was dark, and the door to the chancel was open. The Christmas sacks were sitting in a box on the counting table. Anton pushed the box aside and sat down on the table to watch. Looking on from the dark, it was as though he was eavesdropping on the service—as if the words were being spoken to someone else, not to him. He heard and saw every character, but they had no idea he was there. And he was close, less than ten feet from shepherds, angels, kings, and donkeys. The strangely private performance made Anton watch more closely, more intently than ever before.

Children and adults paraded on and off his private stage. Finally, the church was lit only by candlelight. A woman bearing a lantern took her place on a platform behind the manger. Ginny, divorced from her colorful vocabulary, looked more like the Virgin Mary than anyone would have believed. Tom stood silently behind her. When the pastor read the part about Mary giving birth to her firstborn son, Ginny's mom slipped into the chancel and handed Chelsea to Ginny. It was as though she was presenting her with the most precious gift ever given. The child was wrapped in a beautiful piece of old lace. Ginny took the child and laid her in the manger. She looked down at her daughter with pure admiration, as though the child had been given to her for the first time at that very moment.

The pastor began to speak.

"On that night, God gave the world a magnificent gift. The child was not born just to a Jewish couple in Bethlehem. He was born to the shepherds in the fields. He was born to sorcerers in foreign lands. He was born to a bloodthirsty tyrant in a palace. He was born to children asleep in their beds. He was a gift given not only to people of that age but a gift given to us as well—so that no matter who we are, what we do, or where we live, we can claim this child as our own. There is nothing we could ever do to deserve so great a gift. There is nothing we could ever do to sufficiently express our gratitude. And yet the gift is given."

Pastor Michaels's voice droned on. Anton's eyes drifted shut. In an instant, he was dreaming. He was sitting on a bale of hay at the far end of a dimly lit, empty barn. The cows were gone. Instinctively, Anton rubbed the knee that had robbed him of his herd. His father stood with his back to him, silent and cold. Anton felt the dull ache in his chest as his father walked out of the barn, shaking his head in disgust. Anton felt the shame rising inside. Then he saw the strangest thing. A light began to glow in the door where his father had just disappeared. An old woman with a lantern walked slowly through the door. In her arm rested a beautiful baby. Anton recognized the infant as the Christ Child and, strangely, he longed to hold it.

The woman stopped halfway through the barn and lifted her lantern so she could look at the empty shell. Anton felt afraid. He knew what she was thinking. But the woman didn't say a word. She lowered the lantern, walked silently forward, and placed the beautiful child in Anton's arms. Her voice was warm and assuring. "Anton, you needn't be afraid. Hold onto this child."

Anton wanted to argue, but she touched his lips to silence him. "This child is a gift. A gift to you and to all humankind. He's yours—not because of what you do or what you produce but because of whom God is. This gift does not depend upon you. It depends upon God. God loves you, Anton. Remember that. And one thing more. Anton, you also are a gift—a thing of priceless worth. No matter what you do or where you go, nothing will change that. Cling to this child, Anton, and remember. You are special in God's eyes—not because of what you do but because of who you are. A child of God."

Then the angel put out her foot and stepped on Anton's toe. A frustrated voice spoke to him, "For the love of Jesus, Anton, will you take this baby?"

"What?" Anton said, shaking himself awake.

"The baby, Anton. Would you hold her while I get out of this costume? I'm sweating in places polite ladies don't talk about." She thrust the child into Anton's arms, turned her back to Anton, and stepped out of the costume, revealing her faded blue jeans and baggy Christmas sweater. She threw the costume on the hook on the back of the door and took Chelsea back into her own arms. She opened the door and jerked her head in the direction of the basement. "Come on, Anton. Get your rear in gear. You've got about a verse and a half of 'Joy to the World' to get your butt to the front door with those Christmas sacks."

Anton grabbed the box and started down the stairs. Ginny called from behind him, "And, Anton . . ."

"What?" he asked with more than a hint of impatience in his voice.

"I caught you sleeping in church, you lazy, good-for-nothing sinner man," she mocked.

Anton laughed and moved toward the back as quickly as his old knees could carry him.

I'd like to tell you that Anton never fell asleep in church again, but that would be a lie. Anton is still Pleasant View's premier catnapper, but now when Anton naps, he does so with a smile upon his face.

Timothy Benson: Shepherd King

December 25, 1991

As long as Timothy Benson had been at Pleasant View Lutheran Church, the third graders got first dibs on being the Three Kings. Sure, it didn't always work out. Sometimes there weren't enough third graders. Let's face it. Sometimes there weren't any third graders, and then the older kids got dibs. But when there were third graders, they were the kings!

Now, at last, Timothy Benson was a third grader. At last, Timothy Benson—by all that was right and good in the universe— would inherit the crown. He would be the one wearing the purple velvet robe made from the auditorium curtain salvaged from the high school (before they tore it down about two consolidations ago). He would be the one wearing the Burger King crown covered with aluminum foil and gold-painted macaroni. He would be the one carrying the jewelry box donated to the pageant by Pastor Jacobson's wife in 1973.

But Pastor Loeson had a different idea. Sometime back in October, Loeson went to Rapid City on a continuing education event. There, his colleagues brought it to his attention that he was the sole surviving pastor in South Dakota under the age of seventy who still allowed the Three Kings to be part of the Christmas program. Bruce Peterson—known without affection as Pete the Pontificator—said, "The supposed regal identity of the magi is a sham propagated by the romanticized historiography of some nineteenth-century Episcopalian hymnist. In reality, we know neither the number nor origin of these soothsaying seers. Most likely, they were merely a tribe of Zoroastrian astrologers migrating in the direction of some cosmological irregularity. There is not textual documentation that would allow a real theologian to include them in the midst of the crèche menagerie."

Pastor Loeson wasn't sure he was smart enough to know what Pastor Peterson was talking about, but he certainly was smart enough to know not to ask. The other pastors scolded, shamed, and ribbed him so much that he made a personal vow that this year, there would be no kings.

Timothy Benson had a slightly different worldview. In his mind, he had suffered a good deal of what he considered to be public denigration, waiting for his turn to be king. He had mooed through a hole cut for his face in a cardboard cow. He had sweated through flaccid woolen sheep ears and uncomfortably rigid, garland-covered coat-hanger angel's wings. He had even played the back half of Mary's donkey. Twice he appeared in his mother's bathrobe, his father's dish towel, and his sister's jump rope as a motley shepherd in the field. But through it all, he had not complained. He had been patient. Because he knew that one day, he would be a king. Each year, he put in his time, driven by this regal dream.

On the Sunday before Christmas (when Betty, the church secretary, handed out the assignments), Timothy looked to see which of the Three Kings he would be. He looked twice. "Mrs. Olson!" he cried. "These are the wrong parts. It says here we're shepherds. We've been shepherds for the last two years. This year, we're supposed to be kings. Somebody must have gotten the sheets mixed up."

Mrs. Olson disappeared into the office. In a minute, she reappeared with Pastor Loeson right behind her. Just from the way the pastor was putting on his sport coat, Timothy could tell this was not going to be good news.

"Hello, Timothy. Mrs. Olson said you had a question about the Christmas program."

"Well, yeah. I was wondering why it says we're supposed to be shepherds. I mean, every year, the third graders get to be the kings."

Pastor Loeson really didn't think anyone would notice the change. All he wanted to do was to save face with his theologically astute colleagues. Now he found himself in a liturgical face-off with a blue-eyed ten-year-old that he knew he could not win with dignity. Inside his head, he scrambled like a soon-to-be-sacked quarterback. What did that windbag Peterson say?

"Ah, you're right, Timothy. It used to be that the third graders were the kings. But that was a mistake. There weren't any kings in the barn the night Jesus was born."

He watched Mrs. Olson's eyes grow huge at the heresy.

"I mean, they really didn't show up till much later."

Timothy squinted his eyes. He asked the question with bottom-line clarity. "Then when will we get to be kings?"

Pastor Loeson bent down and pulled a piece of lint from his trousers, trying to be nonchalant. Under his breath, he wished he knew some liturgically correct curse to mail to Pete the Pontificator. "Well, you know, Tim, that's a really good question. Actually, the kings weren't kings at all. Um . . . well . . . if you want to know the truth, they were Zoroastrian astrologers, you know, like psychics and all that. Do you know what I mean?"

Timothy knew exactly what the pastor meant. The third grade class was about to get gypped. They were being demoted to field hands. The pastor rambled on, but Timothy didn't hear a word.

"So you see, Timothy, the really important guys were the shepherds, and that's what I want you to be. And look, you can even wear the cool costumes you wore last year."

It was too much for ten-year-old ears to hear. Timothy turned around. He could feel the tears coming, and he didn't want to give this black-shirted ogre the satisfaction of seeing him cry. He walked out of the sanctuary, down the stairs, and into the bathroom. He put his arms straight down at his sides and made fists, determined not to let the tears come out. When the tears finally stopped pushing against the corners of his eyes, he made a vow with himself.

"No matter what old man Loeson says, I am going to be a king."

It was Christmas Eve and Michael Loeson was at his desk, seated uncomfortably on the horns of a dilemma. He felt for all the world like some kind of Christmas troll. On the radio was one of those trite Hallmark commercials, reminding him that Christmas was the season of giving. He could still see the tiny shoulders of the Benson boy as he stomped down the aisle of the church. He wadded up the sheet of paper that was supposed to contain his sermons and started over again for what seemed like the hundredth time. Liturgical correctness fit him like a camel-hair shirt.

At home, Timothy Benson undertook a clandestine operation. The painfully familiar bathrobe, dish towel, and jump rope lay on his bed. Under the bed was his real costume. In the attic, he found a box marked College. From it he took his mother's mood ring and a gold medallion from the hip pocket of his father's bell-bottomed jeans. The medallion hung from a heavy gold-colored chain and had a deep-purple stone in the middle of it. He grabbed a headband made of some kind of silver metallic fabric braided together with a rich wine-colored cloth. He found another box marked Special Occasions, but he couldn't identify any of the lacy undergarments in that box, and he was pretty sure that neither his mother (nor anyone else's mother for that matter) ever wore anything like that. He quickly put it away and tried to pretend he never saw it. He stole a bunch of dress-up necklaces from his sister's room and stuffed them into the leather marble bag his uncle Dan had given him for Christmas two years ago. From the cedar closet, he borrowed a red satin maternity top his mother wore when she was pregnant with his little sister and a shiny patent-leather belt. Even with the belt cinched up tight around his waist the scarlet garment hung well below his knees. As he looked in the mirror, he looked as fine as any king who had ever traversed the desert.

He was ready. On the outside he would appear to be a stupid old shepherd, just like his stupid old pastor wanted. But inside the false façade, where it really counted, he was a king dressed in the finest raiment.

The time for the Christmas program came. All the parents were in their seats. Timothy carried his costumes in a red duffel. He slipped into the bathroom, locked the door, and got dressed. First he put on his real costume, the regal attire of a king: the royal red vestment, the shimmering gold medallion, the rich silver-and-wine headband crown. He stuffed the leather marble bag of jewels into his black patent-leather belt that held his imperial apparel in place. Over all of this, he placed the shabby trappings of a shepherd. He held his father's tattered old bathrobe closed with two bent safety pins. He put the dish towel over his head, stuffing its edges over and under the headband crown. It wasn't too stable, but at least it hid the glint of his headdress. At the last minute, he threw the dirty, unraveling jump rope cincture back in his bag. "Even a flea-bitten shepherd wouldn't wear that," he told himself.

As the program progressed, group by group, the children took their places in the living Nativity scene. An adult Mary and Joseph came in the midst of the group with a tiny baby wrapped in beautiful piece of lace. All were silent as the light went out and one of the children rang her finger cymbals, the cue for the entrance of the Christmas angel. All eyes turned to the back of the church, toward the heavy oaken doors that were about to burst open so the Christmas angel could make her stately walk to the front of the church, carrying the light of Christmas in her hands.

It was then that Timothy saw the lost sheep. A tiny preschooler with droopy woolen ears stood cowering in front of the towering doors. The little lamb had somehow been separated from the flock and now was frozen in fear as the lights went out. In a moment, the weighty doors would swing open and crush the tiny ewe lamb against the end of the last pew. Timothy looked about, frantically thinking that certainly an adult would notice the unfolding drama, but no one moved.

He had no idea how it happened, but suddenly Timothy found himself walking down the long aisle toward the child. As he bent over to pick up the child, he felt the safety pins give way and his robe fell open, exposing his inner costume. He picked up the child and instinctively the child put her arm around Timothy's shoulder. For the sake of security, she grabbed the dish towel, and it too gave way, unveiling Timothy's shiny crown. At the same moment, the baggy bathrobe fell off his shoulder, and Timothy's regal attire was fully exposed.

Timothy carried the sheep to the front of the church, hoping no one would notice, but Pastor Loeson noticed. At first he looked confused, but soon, the glimmer of recognition brightened his face. Fortunately, he was able to quiet himself so that he did not blurt out "Take that Peterson" like his heart wanted him to.

No one else seemed to notice. They turned to watch the beautiful Christmas angel carrying the Christmas lantern down the aisle. They all sang "Silent Night" together, and all but the Holy Family found their way to their seats.

Michael climbed onto the pulpit. He looked down at his prepared manuscript and then slid it under the Bible. He flipped through the pages of the old Bible for a moment and then read the story of the magi coming to visit Jesus. When he finished, he read again this verse: "And you, Bethlehem, in the land of Judah, are by no means least among the rulers of Judah; for from you shall come a ruler who is to shepherd my people Israel."

The pastor began to speak, but for the most part, his words simply melted into the holiness of the evening and no one really heard them. No one except Timothy. This was what he heard:

"I made a mistake. I once told someone that there was no king present in the stable that first Christmas Eve. I was wrong. There was indeed a king present. It's just that no one recognized him. His name was Jesus. That night, they did not recognize him because he was a child and, of course, foolish people that we are, we expect nothing of children. That is sad.

"But even when he grew to be a man, they still did not recognize him as the king he was. They did not recognize him because he was a king disguised as a lowly shepherd, more concerned with recuing lost sheep than with exercising authority or wielding earthy power. He preferred carrying a sheep on his shoulders to carrying a scepter in his hand.

"Even in his last days, the days he truly proved himself to be a king, they didn't recognize him. They mocked him by putting a purple robe on his shoulders and a crown of thorns on his head. They labeled his cross with a placard reading *The King of the Jews* And they laughed. They laughed because they didn't know that compassion is the finest attribute of a king. They laughed because they didn't know that real kings look more like shepherds than heads of state. They didn't know that real kings are as gifted at caring for their subjects as they are at sending their subjects to war.

"We really should have known. The prophet foretold it. He said a king would come who would be a shepherd to his people Israel. You see, he was a shepherd on the outside, but inside he was the most kingly king the world had ever known. It seems there must be a lesson in this for us. Sometimes, feeding the sheep is more important than being liturgically correct. Sometimes, being compassionate is more important than looking good in the public eye. Sometimes, the real kings are hidden all around us, imitating the love of the King of Kings who came disguised in the nurturing spirit of a shepherd."

I don't know if Timothy Benson understood what Pastor Loeson was talking about. Pastors are seldom smart enough to say things in a way that children can really understand. What's more, Timothy was probably too busy trying to figure out how he was going to explain to his mother why he was wearing her blouse. But I would be willing to bet that next year, the kings will be back in the program. I'll be the first to admit that according to academic authorities, they may not belong there, but I'll bet they'll be there just the same. And I'll bet you my piece of pecan pie that one of them will be Timothy Benson, the shepherd king.

The Death of Ruby Green

December 25, 1992

Pastor Loeson didn't know if he should feel sad or mad. It had been that kind of month.

It seemed to him that every year it got harder and harder to find an infant to play the part of the Christ Child in the living Nativity at the church. In the first place, there just weren't that many babies born in the Pleasant View congregation. In the second place, there weren't many parents who would take on the task of pretending to be the Holy Family in front of a church full of pious Lutherans. Anyone who spent more than fifteen minutes listening to Marguerite Oland gossip in the Bungalow Café knew the dangers of the role.

That's why Pastor Loeson decided to ask a Methodist couple. So, it wasn't long after Sarah and Peter Wentworth gave birth to their baby boy that Pastor Loeson was at their door. Edith Thurmer was really the one that Pastor Loeson had to thank for the availability of the Wentworths in the first place. Edith was the wife of Julius Thurmer, the Methodist pastor. Five years ago, shortly after they moved to town, Edith published a "Spousal Bull" declaring that First Methodist would not offer a midnight Christmas Eve service. "My husband spent the first forty years of our marriage away from home when the clock struck twelve ringing in Christmas," she said. "He'll be spending the next forty years at home with me." Pastor Thurmer was not one to argue with what generally proved to the irrefutable logic of his wife; and the long and the short of it was that Sarah, Peter, and their beautiful brown-eyed son, Daniel, were free for the Christmas Eve midnight service.

On Tuesday at the Bungalow Café, Pastor Loeson mentioned his success. On Wednesday, Marguerite Oland cornered him at the Christian Martyrs' holiday brunch and asked him point blank if Jesus was really going to be a Methodist this year. Pastor Loeson tried to say yes in the most nonchalant way a man can when he's got a glass snack tray balanced on his knee and an overzealous saint breathing down his neck. Marguerite paused and spoke in her quiet, concerned voice.

"Well, perhaps it's for the best. Maybe because of this experience, the child will grow up to be a buffer against the blatant liberalism of those Methodists." She looked around to see if anyone was listening and then whispered in a conspiratorial way, "You know, Pastor, they only have one service on Christmas Eve, and that's at five in the afternoon before the sun has hardly set. What is more, I heard they had to cancel the late service because the pastor's wife demanded it. Well, I don't mind telling you, I don't think there is any room in the body of Christ for pushy women."

Pastor Loeson was about to answer when he heard the phone ring. He excused himself, thanking God for the grace that saved him from saying the words that were forming in the reptilian part of his brain. The phone was the county care facility. Ruby Green, the woman who had so lovingly donated a lacy cloth for the baby Jesus to lie upon, had taken a turn for the worse.

Since the winter of 1990, Ruby Green lived in the care facility. One cold morning in the middle of that winter, Frank Olson found Ruby huddled up next to an old tractor tire in his alleyway corncrib. After he got her warmed up, he took her to her home and found her house smelling like an outhouse, piled to the ceiling with the prizes she had been collecting from the street.

Frank and Pastor Loeson took her out to a place in the country they used to call The County Farm. Upstairs in the old red-bricked two-story building, the men all lived in huge open wards with hardwood floors and steel beds covered with handmade quilts. The women all lived with roommates in little rooms on the first floor. Everyone had a roommate except Ruby. She lived alone in the little room next to the nurses' station that was formerly used for exams back when doctors made house calls.

Michael went to see her every month, but he had to admit that at first he felt a little bit afraid of the crazy old woman. Then one day, on about his fifth visit, Ruby pulled him into her little room and shut the door behind him. She motioned for him to bend his ear down close. "Pastor Loeson," she said, looking over her shoulder at the closed door. "This place is great. You're not going to believe this, but they think I'm crazy." She laughed her high-pitched Halloween laugh. "They give me whatever I want. That's how I got this private room. Here, watch this." She went to the door, kicked it a half dozen times with her heavy leather boots, then stepped back and held her head in her hands, moaning in mock pain. In an instant, the door sprung open and a nervous aide rushed in. "Oh my god, not again!" she cried, examining Ruby's eyes to see if they were dilated. "Pastor, couldn't you stop her? She's going to kill herself banging her head against the door like that. Ruby, you sit here in this chair. I'll get you something warm to drink." The aide rushed out of the room.

Ruby's eyes twinkled as she winked at Michael. "It works every time. Sometimes I even get ice cream. My mom used to do the same thing to me. But once, she kicked the door too hard and stubbed her toe. I nearly peed my pants laughing when I found out what she was doing." On that day, Pastor fell in love with Ruby Green. Even at her craziest, Ruby was a good listener. At her best, she was the wisest woman Pastor Loeson had ever met. Her ability to loosen her grasp on the cold realities of sanity made her the perfect refuge for a pastor who all too often overrated the necessity of a sound mind.

On Wednesday, when Pastor Loeson pulled into the parking lot at the care facility, there was already an ambulance sitting out front next to Frank Olson's truck. When Michael got to her room, the ambulance drivers were arguing with Ruby. She had been sick in bed for three days. She wouldn't eat. She wouldn't drink. She wouldn't take her medicine. She let them lift her onto the gurney, but when they tried to zip her into the bag-like warmer, she panicked. With the strength of Samson, she jumped from the gurney and backed into a corner. After a lot of talking, Pastor Loeson wrapped her in her mother's quilt and she let the EMTs lift her back onto the gurney. Pastor Loeson held her tiny claw-like hand while they buckled the safety restraints. When he tried to leave her so that he could follow the ambulance in his car, she refused to let go. Frank said he'd drive the pastor's car to the hospital, and his wife Betty could pick him up later.

Ruby didn't say another intelligible word for the rest of the stay. She just lay there, looking deep into Pastor Loeson's eyes, shaking her head no. The pastor stayed with her until she finally fell asleep and let his hand go. At two in the morning, he got a call that she was beside herself again. She had pulled out all the tubes. After he got there, they managed to give her something to quiet her. Pastor stood by her bed and watched until she just gave up the fight.

When the funeral director came to pick her up, he said the only time he had left for a funeral was Christmas Eve morning. Pastor Loeson stumbled home to bed and got up at eight o'clock to toll the bell for Ruby. That was the last he slept. On the morning of Christmas Eve, the funeral director showed up with the casket at 9:00 a.m. He and Pastor Loeson moved aside all the props for the Christmas pageant to make room for the casket in the front of the church.

Pleasant View Lutheran Church is graceful about death. No matter who it is that dies, all of them always come to the funeral. Ruby's funeral was not different. Everyone in the parish was there. Somehow, Pastor Loeson limped through a sermon and sat back down in his big oak chair with the red velvet cushion on the seat and the back. As the congregation sang "How Great Thou Art," Pastor Loeson caught himself staring at the casket standing irreverently in front of the church, plugging the center aisle. He couldn't believe she was gone.

The lunch after the funeral was standard. Sandwiches made out of a beef salad they called Funeral Spread, red Jell-O, and a smorgasbord of cakes. Marguerite and the Christian Martyrs served. By two o'clock, the church was cleaned and empty.

At six thirty, Pastor Loeson met with the Wentworth family and directed them toward his secretary, Betty Olson, Frank's wife. She said she'd see to it that they all got dressed. Five minutes later, Betty was back in the office. "I need the blanket," she said, brushed past him, pulled out a box marked Ruby's Gift, and disappeared out the door.

Maybe because he was tired or maybe because he was just plain sad, Pastor Loeson felt numb through the entire Christmas program. If you would have asked him the next day what his sermon was about, he would have no idea what he said. Given the quality of his sermon, that was perhaps merciful. Throughout the service, he just sat in his chair and stared at the place where the casket had been. Now, strangely enough, in that exact same place stood the old wooden manger full of its bright-yellow straw.

At one point the lights dimmed and the choir began singing "What Child Is This?" Pastor Loeson fought the heaviness of his eyes. The choir began the second verse,

> Why lies he in such mean estate
> Where ox and ass are feeding?

Pastor Loeson's eyes fluttered and the manger began to swim and melt in front of him. For an instant it disappeared, and there instead of the manger was the casket of Ruby Green. The choir drifted into his dream.

> Good Christian fear; for sinners here
> The silent word is pleading.

The dream continued and the Holy Family made their way down the aisle, carrying the Christ Child so beautifully wrapped in Ruby's greatest treasure. The sweet baby cooed as its mother lovingly carried him. In some terrible place in his mind, Pastor Loeson knew what was going to happen next. He wanted to shout but in his sleep, he could only grunt. The Holy Family approached the gaping casket that sat where the manger should have been. The words of the choir darkened the nightmare.

> Nails, spear shall pierce him through
> The cross he bore for me, for you.

The Holy Family reached the front of the church, and the Virgin Mary bent over Ruby's casket. She took the innocent child and lowered her into the cold steel mouth of the deathbed. The mother stood now with aching, empty arms as she looked down at the newborn lying in death's grip.

Pastor Loeson's eyes snapped wide open. He heart pounded inside of his chest. In the aisle in front of him, Sarah Wentworth was carefully bending over the manger, laying her baby softly in the straw. The choir continued.

> Hail, hail the word made flesh,
> The babe, the son of Mary.

Michael Loeson shook his head and tried to take a deep breath. Somewhere inside of him, a door opened up, and there, in the dark, he silently began to weep. It was too much for one day. It didn't seem right that life and death should be so closely woven together. The birth of a baby and the death of a saint shouldn't touch like that, especially here at Christmas. Especially here with a beautiful little baby in a lovely little manger. It all seems too morbid, too rude for something as special as Christmas. Michael Loeson was thankful for the dark. He crept out of the sanctuary through the sacristy door and went down into the basement to collect himself.

Through some act of divine intervention, Michael Loeson made it through the Christmas greetings at the back door. After he watched the last car crunch down the icy road, he walked back through the church, shutting off lights. In the darkness, he absently pulled a few pieces of straw from the manger and put on his black topcoat. He started to walk toward the parsonage but unconsciously wandered into the frosty cemetery. There, beneath the clear skies and the twinkling stars, he stood over the grave of Ruby Green.

He smiled as he remembered her laughing eyes in the midst of her broken life. And somehow, there, with the Christmas stars overhead and the smell of fresh soil piled on a newly filled grave, it all fit together. Infants, caskets, mangers, and crosses, they were all part of the whole of life. *So this is Christmas,* he thought. *A baby born in the midst of a dying people, a birth that changes everyone's death, and then later, on a cross, a death that changes everyone's life. That's what moved Ruby to present Jesus with her most prized possession. That's why we dare place a casket in the same place we put the manger.*

There, alone, in the wind and the snow, he sang the last verse of the song that haunted him,

> So bring him incense gold and myrrh
> Come peasant, king to own him
> The King of Kings salvation brings.
> Let loving hearts enthrone him.

> Raise, raise, the song on high,
> The Virgin sings her lullaby;
> Joy, joy, for Christ is born,
> The babe, the son of Mary!

Michael took the straw he had plucked from the manger, twisted it into a simple cross, and laid it on the fresh earth of the grave. With that, he turned up the collar of his coat and walked home to celebrate the miracle of Christmas with his family.

Michael Loeson: The Innkeeper

December 25, 1993

Michael Loeson was in more trouble than he'd ever been in before. It all started last summer when Marguerite Oland went to Jamestown, North Dakota, and discovered the Born-Again Christian Consignment Store. The bottom of their sign read "Our inventory is not used; it is reborn." It was there that Marguerite purchased a Lutheran software package called Tidy Desk. The cover of the package quoted a verse from the Living Bible, "God is not one who likes things to be disorderly . . . ." Marguerite said, "Pastor, when I read that verse, I automatically thought of your desk. With a little prayer and this software, maybe even your humble little writing table can proclaim the glory of God."

Michael Loeson booted the software up and discovered a pastoral calling calendar that he thought might actually be of some help to him.

Pastor Loeson had not done well in making his home visits this year. Ever since Ruby Green died, he found it more and more difficult to make his monthly homebound calls. Although he would not admit it, the pain of her death after he had grown so close to her, made him a little gun shy when it came to calling. He didn't know it, but his subconscious had written a pact with his injured heart. It prescribed that he keep his distance from his flock. He was to be more professional. After all, his parishioners were busy. They really didn't need some young pastor coming around and bothering them all the time. He found himself spending more time in his office with pious puttering and less time in the homes of his parishioners. He told his wife that he was trying to be more professional. He didn't know that what he was really trying to be was safe.

Once he got it set up, The Tidy Desk Pastor Calling program worked pretty well. Like most Lutheran systems, it operated on guilt. Every time he turned on the computer, the names of the homebound appeared on the screen. Every hour on the hour, until all the calls were completed, the computer played a verse of "Chief of Sinners though I Be." When he completed a call, a dove with a frightfully joyful, face appeared on the screen.

On the Monday before Christmas, Michael called up the screen with the names of all the homebound. He had a long-running custom of calling on all homebound the week before Christmas. He worked hard on the list. Every night, he tagged the names of the persons he visited in an attempt to stifle the guilt-inspiring hymn. By the day before Christmas Eve, he had called on every name on the screen.

On Christmas Eve morning, he turned on the computer with a flourish, expecting a well-deserved respite from the hymn, but there it was again. He looked at the list of tagged names. There were twenty-five names and twenty-five grinning doves. He scratched his head. Then with fear and trembling, he tapped the Page Down key, and a new page appeared with a single entry on it: "Andrew Gilbertson, Veteran's Home, Sioux Falls, South Dakota."

"Rats!" Michael said. "Now what am I going to do? Sioux Falls is three hours away. I can't make a trip like that. Not today."

But as he spoke, somewhere in the center of his reptilian brain, a fearful image of Marguerite Oland swam into focus. He could feel the flight or fight reflex engage as he imagined her addressing the Christian Martyrs Circle. "I don't know. I guess our pastor is just too busy these days, doing important things like drinking coffee with Mable Trogemann to remember someone as insignificant as an old war hero, wounded and paralyzed for the sake of his country. When I was a child, people like Andrew Gilbertson were important, but today," Michael imagined that Marguerite interrupted herself to express the deepest, most painfully humble and righteous sigh known to Lutheranism before she continued, "today, the world has turned upside down."

Marguerite Oland, the Tidy Desk program, and a double dose of Lutheran guilt allowed Michael Loeson to entertain a ridiculous idea. He said to himself, "It's nine thirty. I can be on the road by ten. In three hours, I'll be in Sioux Falls. That puts me there at one. I spend an hour with Andy, two p.m. Three hours back, I will arrive here at five. I'll still have 2 1/2 hours before the Christmas program at seven thirty."

Michael dashed off a note to his wife. "Had to run a few quick errands. Back by suppertime. See you then. Merry Christmas. PS, I love you."

In about three dozen bounds, he ran out of the church and into the parsonage. He laid the note on the table and pulled out this wallet to see if he had any money. His wallet was empty. He laid his wallet on the table and ran upstairs to the bedroom to get a five-dollar bill out of a Christmas card he received the day before. He stuffed the bill in his front pocket. The phone rang. He answered three questions about the Christmas program and bounded back to the office.

At the church he put a box of bulletins in the narthex and the box of Christmas candy sacks on top of the coat rack. He grabbed his sermon and stuffed it in his parka pocket. He had the strange feeling that he had forgotten something but wasn't sure what. Taking one last look around the office, he flipped off the light. In the darkened room, the screen of the computer seemed to beam across the office at him. He thought about turning it off but then shrugged and slammed the door. Through the thick oaken door, he could hear the computer, ever watchful, beeping out the melody, "Chief of Sinners though I be . . ."

The ride to Sioux Falls was frustrating.

He stopped at the All Nite Made Rite on the west edge of Brookings. In his haste, he failed to notice that the sign had been changed to Ingeborg's House of Tacos. He ordered the *Puerto del Oslo* sub and then spent fifteen minutes watching Ingeborg move back and forth between his sandwich and the intricate recipe taped to the front of the refrigerator beneath a sign that said "I don't do it fast. I do it right." He paid with the five in his front pocket, and Ingeborg counted back every penny.

He pulled out onto the highway just in time to be stopped by the world's longest freight train. When the train was almost past, it came to a slow halt and began backing up to pick up some cars that must have been left on a siding twelve miles up the track in Bruce. Michael slammed his hand against the steering wheel and looked around. Next to the track, there stood an old two-story brick hotel. You could see the damaged bricks where the original sign used to hang. In its place hung a red neon cross with the words *Jesus is Lord* flashing in blue next to it. From the window, a poster proclaimed "Free Soup Every Noon, Free Beds Every Night, Jesus is your friend." An old man in an army-surplus jacket was putting red, white, and blue tinsel garlands around the neon cross. Michael cringed and made a non-repeatable statement about the man's shabby theology and the hotel's shabby clientele. When the train finally passed, he scooted across the tracks and set his face for Sioux Falls.

His visit with Andy was time consuming. They talked for a while and had Communion. When Andy found out Michael had his sermon in his pocket, he made him read the entire homily to him. Afterward, Andy insisted they go to the dining room for eggnog and Christmas cookies. Michael tried to beg off but Andy wouldn't hear it. After his second cookie, Michael looked up from his eggnog, and it was three thirty.

If he left immediately, he would be home by six thirty and only have an hour before the program began. He eased the conversation with Andy to an end and wheeled him back toward his room. In the hallway, Andy introduced Michael to everyone they met. As Michael stopped to put on his gloves he looked at his watch. It was four o'clock. He opened the door and found himself in the midst of a blizzard.

Michael walked back inside to a pay phone. He called his wife.

The content of the phone conversation is not one that lay people should be privy to. Michael delicately explained his whereabouts, and Lorraine took a few moments to explain some of Michael's character flaws to him. She also gave him a few less-than-gentle hints on time management. Let it be said that the wind in the parking lot ran a distant second to the cold blast that came across the phone.

Michael spent a good ten minutes scraping the ice off his windows. He drove ten miles an hour down Minnesota Avenue on his way to the interstate. "It's always worse in town than on the freeway," he told himself. He was wrong. As he pulled unto I-29 North, his car fishtailed and then spun 360 degrees. Michael took two hours to make the sixty-mile drive to Brookings. He pulled off the interstate and drove past the Holiday Inn. Thirty semis and four times that many cars packed the parking lot. A clerk was putting up a big sign in the window: Absolutely No Rooms Left.

On the west edge of town, a highway patrol cruiser blocked the highway. The trooper explained that every road out of town was closed. Michael couldn't believe his ears. He pulled across the street into a gas station. As he slammed his car door he said to himself, "Well at least things can't get any worse than this." He reached into his back pocket to get his wallet, and suddenly, he remembered what he had forgotten. A clear picture of his billfold lying firmly on the kitchen table formed in his mind. He went into the service station and made a collect call home, but no one answered. He tried to call the church, but the line was busy. Mable Trogemann had removed the phone from the hook to make sure the program practice would not be disturbed. He walked back to his car and the clerk locked the station door behind him. One by one, the lights of the station went black.

As Michael drove through town, every restaurant, every gas station, every convenience store, even every church sat darkened and silenced by the ice storm. Michael Loeson began to talk to himself. "What an idiot. I can't believe I tried to make this stupid trip. I can't believe I let an old woman and a computer program intimidate me. I can't believe I left my billfold lying on the kitchen table. I can't believe Mable Trogemann took the phone off the hook again this year so that her precious program practice wouldn't be disturbed. I can't believe what a screw-up I am. I can't belief they let cretins like me walk around on the street. What was I thinking?"

Michael stopped and looked to his right. A red neon cross interrupted his self-assessment. He had less than a quarter of a tank of gas. He had a dollar and sixty-nine cents in his pocket. His stomach growled. He read the sign in the window for a second time, "Free Soup Every Noon, Free Beds Every Night, Jesus is your friend." He took a deep breath, pulled over, shut off his car, and walked in.

Inside, he found his way to what the management called the dining room. He opened the door and stood still to take in the sight. Thirty people were eating supper at long tables. One table held a half dozen men, unshaven, dressed rough, like they had been on the street a long time. They were the stereotypical derelicts he expected. Another table held the old tinsel-hanging man, his wife, and three women in white aprons. They were the born-again fanatics he expected. But the other tables shocked him. They held an assortment of children and their parents. One woman stood with a baby on her hip, talking to a man feeding a toddler on his lap. She looked up, saw him, and called out "Hello!"

Soon the old man and his wife were at his side. He was Brother Bob and she was Anne. Michael explained what had happened and Ann drew her clasped hands up close to her bosom and said, "Well, Rev. Loeson, praise Jesus. I just know you have been sent here to us as a gift from God. This is a holy night." Michael Loeson swallowed hard.

It wasn't long and he was at a table with toasted day-old bread, government-commodity peanut butter, and vegetable soup. While he ate, the old man and his wife began to move between the tables, serving the guests like they were family, holding a baby, laughing with one of the rough-looking men, and easing the tension between two others.

After supper, they all moved into what used to be the lobby of the hotel. An ancient artificial Christmas tree that looked like it had been made of green toilet brushes tottered in one corner of the room. Anne distributed an armful of tattered choir robes; dish towels; red, white, and blue garlands; a purple bedspread; an old baby doll; and a cane. The children became shepherds, kings, angels, and the Holy Family. She reached into the pocket of her apron and pulled out a Gideon's New Testament and handed it to Michael. On cue, he was to read the Christmas story. She handed out a sheath of folded song sheets, plopped down at a Hammond home organ and started to play carols. And the homeless became a choir.

Michael watched as the men, women, and children joined in. He marveled at how easily the forsaken lobby became a sanctuary. He read the story and was filled with awe at how seriously the children took their roles, enacting the holy birth. When the divine drama was over, Brother Bob gathered the children around the feet of his brown, cracked vinyl chair.

"When I was little, my daddy used to try to teach me how to swim. He'd take me down to the creek and tell me to wade out there into the water and start swimming. He'd stand there on the shore and holler and point. I'd splash around and swallow a bathtub full of water and come up coughing and crying, and my daddy would get so mad he couldn't talk. He'd cuss me out and tell me to get my overalls on and get up there and scoop out the barn. I hated it when my daddy got mad, so I tried just as hard as I could, but I just couldn't figure it out.

"Then one summer, my uncle Billy came to stay with us. I really loved Uncle Billy. He was about the best uncle any boy could have. At lunch, Daddy told me Uncle Billy was going to teach me how to swim. I felt sick. I knew I couldn't learn how to swim, and now Uncle Bill was going to be just as mad at me as my daddy was. After lunch, Uncle Billy walked down to the creek with me. He never told me to get in the water. He just got in the water and started swimming around. After a while he calls up to the bank, 'You should come on in here. It's a lot cooler in here than sitting up there in the hot sun.' I waded into the water. All summer long, Uncle Billy and I went down to the creek every day, right after lunch. I watched Uncle Billy swim, and I asked him questions, and he showed me this and that. And you know what? By the time the summer was over, I knew how to swim.

"I told my daddy to come down and watch me, and he smiled from ear to ear when he saw that I knew how to swim. I asked him if he wanted to come in and swim, and he said he couldn't. And I said, 'Why not?' And he said, 'Because I never had an Uncle Billy to teach me how to swim.'

"Christmas is about God being like Uncle Billy. We're all down here on earth trying to figure out how to swim, and God picked Jesus to climb into the creek with us. God sent Jesus down so he could be close to the people. So he could go to the house of a sick little girl and, with just the touch of his hand, make her better.

So he could find some hungry people and break up some bread so they'd have a little something to eat. So he finds a woman all lonely and confused and in real big trouble and stays right by her side no matter what anybody said about her or tried to do to her.

"He was the kind of man that if a snowstorm came up and one of his sheep ran off, he'd leave all the others home, safe in the barn, so that he could go out and find one poor old lost sheep who was just waiting to see him." Brother Bob looked up and winked at Michael Loeson.

I don't know if the children had any idea why Brother Bob was talking about sheep all of a sudden, but Michael Loeson did. He got the point. This old man, with no theological training or professional credentials, was speaking the truth. The sheep were all home, safe in the barn. Christmas didn't depend on his being there. And it didn't depend on fancy programs or spellbinding sermons or tidy desks. It depended on a god who just couldn't stay out of the troubled waters of this world. A god who could find a way even into a crumbling hotel by the side of the tracks in Brookings, South Dakota. A god who could find a way into the life of a frightened, forgetful young pastor who found it painful to love his flock as much as he really loved them. A god who understood a young man who was just trying to silence that hymn, "Chief of Sinners though I Be" that played over and over again in his head. What's more, it was because of Christmas that he knew that he needed to take the risk of getting close to all those who called him pastor and friend. God couldn't keep a civil distance, and if Michael thought about it, neither could he, whether he was a sinner or not.

Later that night, Pastor Loeson called his wife. Once again there were words that are best left unreported. But there was an

"I'm sorry" or two and an "I-forgive-you-but-you-really-owe-me-big-this-time." The service went fine without the pastor being present. Some even thought it went a little better. They included him in their prayers.

Lorraine said there was only one problem. Betty Olson, the church secretary, rushed into the office looking for an extra drop cord for the program. Somehow the pastor's computer got left on, and she accidentally unplugged it. When she plugged it back in, she heard a pop. The computer seemed to be all right, but she couldn't get the Tidy Desk program to boot. If the pastor would just give her the address of the computer store where he bought it, she would be glad to buy him a new copy. She was really embarrassed.

"Tell Betty not worry about it," he said. "I don't think I'll be needing that program anymore."

In the light of day, Pastor Loeson had a safe trip home. He and his wife are still negotiating the terms of his forgiveness, but I think they'll work it out. It has something to do with a shopping trip to Sioux Falls, a nice dinner out, and an overnight at one of those hotels that specialize in service. Pastor Loeson said Lorraine could pick the date and the restaurant, but he already had the perfect hotel in mind.

Peter Trump: The Grump

December 25, 1994

Peter Trump is a grump. Everybody at Pleasant View Lutheran Church knows it. He was the sole reason there had never been a unanimous vote cast at a Pleasant View congregational meeting. Peter always voted "No!" He figured that if everyone else was for something, that was reason enough for him to be against it.

Peter hadn't always been a grump. In the early days, Peter was not as grumpy as he was serious. He was the only one in the first grade who went home and actually studied when his teacher announced they were going to have an eye test. He never told an elephant joke. He never stuck a frog in Nancy McGuire's lunch box even though she desperately deserved it. And as far as Mabel Trogemann, Sunday school superintendent, knew, he was the only four-year-old in the history of Pleasant View Lutheran Church who didn't believe in Santa Claus.

Peter's seriousness took a turn for the worse when Peter was in the second grade. Peter's dad, Augie, was as jocular and fat as Peter was thin and serious. Augie's wife, Ruthanne, was just the same. Peter was the only child, and with all that warmth and jocularity around, Peter decided somebody in the family had to take things seriously. He nominated himself.

At about the same time, Augie pushed his propensity to consume rinderwurst and Johnnycakes to the limit and ended up in the hospital with a heart attack. The whole affair sent little Peter into a tailspin, and when he came out of it, he took things five times more seriously than before his father's brush with death. At first, Augie tried to kid Peter out of his seriousness. But the more jovial Augie got, the more Peter felt like he needed to be serious, and the two became caught in a never-ending dance.

To hear his parents tell it, Peter's seriousness aged into downright orneriness about the time he moved back home from college in 1971. The change kind of surprised them. For the two years preceding his graduation, Peter's dark mood appeared to go into remission while he was under the influence of a certain young coed there. But when Peter moved back home, his cantankerousness ripened like a crock of limburger cheese. Peter the Serious became Peter the Grump.

Peter works out at the Four Corners Hardware Store with his dad. The store had two claims to fame. For travelers, it was famous for its roasted nuts. There wasn't a traveling salesman in South Dakota who drove past Four Corners without stopping for a bag of toasted cashews. But the farmers of that region came for far more important reasons. From the very beginning, the Trumps bought everything in bulk. This perpetual overstocking was a great blessing to the penny-pinching farmers of the region.

It kept their machinery running for decades beyond its planned obsolescence. Back in 1930, when Oscar Legried needed a pitman arm assembly for his McCormick Deering horse-drawn mower, old Sigert Trump ordered five of them. In 1985, Four Corners still had two of them. Last year, Roland Nelson needed a swinging drawbar for his Farmall F-14, so he drove all the way down from Baldhill, North Dakota, and Augie sold it to him at its original retail price. He still had a case of wicks for the lantern Magda's grandpa gave her when she was just sixteen years old, and Magda's well over eighty.

Augie would have retired a long time ago if he weren't afraid of the store losing all its customers to Peter's orneriness. You see, the only way the Four Corners kept going was out of the pure benevolence of its patrons. Everybody loved Augie, so they made it a point to patronize the store, even though it was a bit inconvenient. But nobody loved Peter. Augie knew that left to his own devices, Peter would bury the store in less than eighteen months. Case in point was Peter's treatment of the Christmas treat bags. Somehow—no one is quite sure how—Peter got elected to be congregation treasurer. As such, he was responsible for ordering the treat sacks presented to the children at the Christmas Eve worship services. The treat bags had always been the same: one cup of roasted-in-the-shell peanuts, one apple or one orange (whichever was on sale), one candy cane, and two red-and-white ribbon candies. Last week, Pastor Loeson got a thank you note from the food bank in Brookings. Peter had decided that the people of Pleasant View had fallen victim to a national conspiracy to spoil the children of our nations by over-indulging them at Christmastime. Instead of ordering treat sacks, he sent the money off to the Feed the World Fund. Pastor Loeson was furious, and so was Augie. Augie told the pastor that the least he could do was to provide each of the children with a bag of home-roasted peanuts.

Things came to a head on Christmas Eve when Augie, Ruthanne, and Peter were putting the bags of nuts into the trunk of Augie's Buick. Peter did a quick count and realized that they were two dozen bags short. Augie said, "Oh yeah, I ran out of nuts so I put a gunny sack of green peanuts into the roaster. I was talking to Anton Anderson, and I guess I forgot all about it."

Peter flew into a rage about his father's stupidity and sputtered off to the store to pick up the rest of the peanuts and to keep the entire complex from burning down. When Peter got to the hardware store, he could smell the charred remains of the peanuts. He slammed his car door twice, once for his dad and once for the burned nuts. He went into the store and got more green peanuts, went out back, dumped out the burned nuts, put the green ones in, and then went back inside to wait. While he was waiting, he realized that there were only five of the small paper bags left. In a rage, he threw his coat down on the counter and kicked the trash can.

Across the back of the old building was a long lean-to that Sigert Trump had added for storage. It had never been used for display, so it wasn't heated. This is where they kept everything that they "couldn't think of any place else to keep it." The only way in or out of the old lean-to was through a thick oak door that had originally been the back door of the store. The door was always kept open because somewhere along the line, the key to the door had been lost, and if the door became locked the only way out was to take the door off of the hinges.

Peter looked in every nook and cranny of the main store for paper sacks, and when he had exhausted his exploratory options, he walked back into the lean-to. He folded his arms against the cold and started to poke around the dimly lit lean-to. Finally he saw the bundle of sacks poking out of a shelf high up behind the heavy oak door. He tried to swing the door out of the way, but someone had stopped the door open by jamming a screwdriver, wedged in place by a hammer, under the door. They were really stuck and Peter scraped his knuckles on the rough floorboards trying to get them out. "Who the hell put those in there? That's not where they belong." Self-righteously, he carried them both to the bucket of tools by the cash register and threw them in.

He carefully swung the door partway shut so that he could get a stool in place to reach the bags. He stood on his tiptoes, and when he stretched to reach the bundle, the stool lurched on the uneven floorboards. Peter lost his balance and swung around so that the bundle took out the lone light bulb swinging from a socket in the ceiling. Fortunately, even in the complete darkness, he was able to land on his feet and steady himself against something that gave a little and then became as solid as a rock. Unfortunately, the solid thing against which his back rested was the old oak door. The last thing Peter heard as he pushed himself to an upright position was the click of the lock.

Peter threw down the sacks and rattled the latch. He kicked the door. He flicked on the Bic lighter in his pocket and walked around the lean-to until he found a candle. He tried to pull the pins out of the hinges but they were rusted in place. He slapped his forehead as he realized that the only way to get those pins out was with the hammer and screwdriver that he had dutifully placed in a bucket by the cash register. "Dammit! I should have let this place burn down."

Peter Trump the Grump sat down on the floor and leaned against the oak door. The wind that whistled in between the floorboards was painfully cold. He wrapped his arms around himself to keep warm. As he sat there, he began to shiver.

When he could take it no longer, Peter got up off the floor and—with candle in hand—walked to the far end of the lean-to looking for something to keep him warm. There on another high shelf, he saw the sleeve of his grandfather's old Santa Claus suit hanging out of a box. He got the box down and stood silently as an internal debate raged in his head. On the one hand, he was cold and this Santa Claus suit certainly did look warm. On the other hand, he was a grump and had been a grump for a very long time. As a confirmed grump, it seemed almost sacrilegious even to consider vesting himself in a Santa suit, no matter how cold he was.

He pushed the suit aside and began to dig around in the box. In the bottom of the carton rested his grandfather's rusty old ice-fishing tackle box. Inside the tackle box were three Minnesota Tear Drops, two Swedish Pimples, and a pint of peppermint schnapps. Breaking the seal on the bottle of schnapps, Peter quickly devised an alternative heating program. After his fourth snort from the bottle, putting on the Santa Claus suit seemed like a viable option. After the seventh snort, it seemed downright mandatory. With a great deal of determination, Peter put on the suit. One more snort convinced him that he would be warmer with the hat on. Having donned the hat, a celebrative pull on the bottle gave birth to the realization that his chin would be warmer covered by a Santa beard.

Fully comforted by a Santa Suit and a belly full of peppermint schnapps, Peter was in an exploratory mood. He climbed up on the stool to see what else was hidden on the top shelf. He pulled down an enormous Charmin box and plopped it on the floor. It was filled with assorted boxes stuffed with receipts dating back to the fifties and more than a few ancient rolls of toilet paper. Peter rummaged through the assortment until, way in the bottom of the box, he found a red shoebox with a single word written on it: Ellie.

Peter reached in and took the box with trembling hands. He sat down on the floor and laid the box in his lap. He had thrown this box away over twenty years ago. Apparently someone had rescued it from the fire. Pulling the candle close, he took the lid off and inside he saw every letter Ellen had ever sent him. He thumbed through the box to the letter in the back. He opened it and began to read. He really didn't need to read it. After twenty years, he still had every word memorized, even though he spent every waking moment fighting to forget them.

Petey,

> *I have never felt so confused in all my life. I have never loved anyone as much as I love you. All I can think about is your quiet, reluctant smile, your warm hand in mine, and your strong arms around me. I know that you love me. You can't deny that. That's why, I don't know why it so hard for you to let me in. I don't know what you mean when you say, "Loving you is a risk I just can't take." I know that I could be happy wherever I was as long as I was with you. But I can't wait any longer. And I can't write any more letters knowing I'll never get an answer. It seems like it has always been like that . . . .*

*Me doing the loving . . . . You doing the running. I'm
taking the job in Boston but I would give anything just
to be with you at Four Corners. The saddest thing is,
Petie, I always knew that you were the one.*

I love you.

Ellie

Peter never wrote back. He wouldn't take the chance. If his
father's illness had taught him nothing else, it taught him one
thing: "Don't get too close. Don't allow yourself to care or you
might get hurt." For a couple of years, he let himself slip with
Ellie. But the more he cared for Ellie, the more he found him
himself caring for others as well. He felt those warm feelings of
compassion welling up within him. But then his mind would go
back to the second grade. He'd see the back of that ambulance
hauling his dad down to Brookings, and it was more than he could
take. He never knew when the bastard would leave him for good.
And he knew that he'd never get over that abandonment. So he
spent twenty years pushing people away, not getting involved, and
keeping safe.

Now, twenty years later, he felt the pain like he never felt it
before. Usually, he was able to push it down, but now, in the dark,
on the floor of a storage shed on Christmas Eve, the pain came
bubbling to the surface. And it didn't come alone. It came with
the fear of a second-grade boy who thought his dad was going to
die. It came with the agony of about thirty years' worth of doing
whatever he had to do to keep his distance from everybody so
that he would never feel that afraid again. It came with a dull,

hollow feeling of not daring to believe in anything for fear that he would be taken off guard again by something or someone as wonderful as Ellie.

Peter reached into the Charmin box, pulled out one of the old rolls of toilet paper, and blew his nose. He had forgotten how lonely he felt. He was too busy being nasty to think about loneliness. He was so busy slapping up protective fences that he never had time to look around and see that he was the only one left inside the fences. He spent his whole life trying to protect himself from the feeling he was having right now. A life of strategic defensiveness and one slip, one stupid old letter, and now the very thing he feared enveloped him.

Peter dropped the toilet paper roll back into the box and a stack of cardboard folders caught his eye. He took another swig from the bottle and examined the folders. They were an assortment of Lenten dime folders from the '60s. Their covers were adorned with a variety of pictures in deep tones of purple and back. Most of the pictures were standard Lenten fare. Jesus on the cross. Jesus in the garden. Jesus in the upper room. But one picture made him stare. He held the candle up to get a closer look.

It was the strangest picture he had ever seen. At first, it looked only like a picture of the baby Jesus standing on his mother's lap. But a closer look revealed something far more bizarre. The little figure on Mary's lap was not a chubby-cheeked cherub like Peter had seen in his Sunday school books. This infant had the lean face of a man with a stubbly beard. His face was wizened and furrowed. And the infant-man pointed to a full-sized crown of thorns lying on his mother's lap, just waiting for him to grow into.

There was something very powerful about the eyes of this Jesus. They were deep set and heavily creased. In those eyes, Peter saw the depth of this child-man's weariness. It was the weariness of travel. It was not just the weariness of traveling from Nazareth to Bethlehem or even the weariness of traveling from Bethlehem to distant Egypt. It was the kind of weariness that could have come only from traveling from eternity down to into the painful circumstance of being human. And somehow, it was a weariness that looked all too familiar. It was the weariness of a second grader who lived his whole life trying to live the bargain of good behavior in exchange for his father's life. It was the weariness of a young man with this whole life ahead of him who didn't dare to fall in love for the fear that it might hurt too much. It was the weariness of a grown man who knew the temptation of spending every waking moment acting like a grump rather than allowing anyone too close. It was the weariness of wearing flesh rather than being in some distant spirit world.

But there was something else peculiar about this child-man. As worn and scarred as this baby looked, he also looked very much at home. He stood with one hand resting gently on his mother's shoulder as though he had been there with her all along. The ease of his stance made it look as though this long journey into human flesh was not so much a downward journey as it was a journey home, a journey back to the place he had always longed to be. He stood beside that gruesome crown of thorns as calm and ready as though all these pains and indignities were simply a part of being who and where he was meant to be. He was at home in the messiness of being human—the painful, risky, threatening messiness of living among a people he loved and was willing to die for even if it was a death at their hands.

Peter pictured his own life. He felt the battle he fought against living in the midst of this human mess. Born of a human parent who dared to nearly die. Caught in fragile relationships that no one seemed to take seriously enough. Bruised by encounters with those other flawed human beings. And here was this Christ Child looking for all the world as though this was the life he had chosen to live.

All too aware of this human mess, Peter did what was, for him, a very uncommon thing. He bowed his head and prayed. I don't know what he prayed. I'm not even sure if Peter knew what he prayed. I don't even know if the prayer had words. But he prayed something from the very bottom of his very human heart. And he prayed with all the earnestness that the eyes of the child-man evoked. And somehow the prayer made a difference.

Peter placed all the items back in the Charmin box and put it up on the shelf. In a joyful frenzy, he started snapping open the small paper treat bags, setting them in a semicircle around him with the candle right in the middle of the hoard. He ran to the far end of the shed and took down a huge box marked Fisher's Best. The box was an assortment of the highest quality of fancy factory-roasted nuts. Quickly, Peter opened package after package of filberts, cashews, hazelnuts, and almonds. He poured the nuts into row after row of the treat bags, until he was surrounded by nearly seventy-five bags.

Now all the time that Peter Trump was having his schnapps-assisted spiritual awakening, Augie Trump was waiting nervously at the church. Finally, he decided he'd better stop out at the store and see what was happening with Peter. Walking into the store, he took a quick look around and then noticed the huge oak door was closed.

There was nothing in life as we know it that could have prepared Augie for what he saw on the other side of that door.

What he expected to find was Peter Trump the Grump storming around the lean-to trying to find a way out. What he actually found looked instead like the cover of a Hallmark card. There before him, kneeling on the floor, was Santa Claus, dressed in full array, filling bags of treats for all the good little boys and girls.

Augie usually has something clever to say, but frankly, this scene left him speechless. He shook his head a couple of times to clear his vision and then said, "Peter, is that you?" Peter was so busy with his task that he never heard the door swing open. When he heard his father, he simply looked up and said, "Well, don't just stand there. Get out front and get some of those boxes. We've got to hurry if we're going to get these to the church before the program is over."

When Santa speaks to you on Christmas Eve, it's really not polite to ask questions. Augie just did what he was told. They loaded up the bags and hightailed it to church.

Peter, preoccupied with the task at hand and still somewhat sedated by the schnapps, didn't remember what he was wearing until he saw his reflection in the new glass doors on the front of the church. He stopped dead in his tracks, but it was too late. Inside the church, a river of child-sized shepherds and angels spied Santa Claus coming at them with a box full of goodies and cascaded in his direction. He met them at the door and started to fill dozens of miniature hands with some of the best nuts in four counties.

Pastor Loeson stood at the top of the stairs and gaped, unable to believe his eyes as he saw a man who looked an awful lot like Peter Trump the Grump playing Santa Claus.

No one ever asked Peter what happened. They were afraid to. And Peter never said. He was still enough of a grump to enjoy knowing that only he knew something that everybody else at Pleasant View Lutheran Church was dying to find out. He still wore his humanity like an ill-fitted porcupine-quill sweater, but occasionally, just occasionally, a neighbor might catch Peter in an act of compassion. Augie was surprised to find a few long-distance calls to Boston on the phone bill, but he never got around to asking about it. Peter still holds the record for *no* votes at Pleasant View congregational meetings, but now, at least when he registers his vote, you can catch the smile in his eyes.

Lyle Hegland: Servant of God
December 25, 1995

Pleasant View is an open country church plopped down in the middle of a wheat field on the vast plains of South Dakota. There's not much out that way, so on a sunny fall afternoon, the white wood frame stands out like a lighthouse against the tans and grays of the prairie. Anton Anderson looked out across those plains on the Friday after Thanksgiving and could see Lyle Hegland's pick-up from about a mile and a half away. Lyle just turned forty-nine and was celebrating his thirtieth anniversary as Pleasant View's janitor.

Lyle was just finishing putting out Pleasant View's newest acquisition: a plastic lighted Nativity set. Anton bought the whole set at a farm sale up in North Dakota for fifteen bucks. It was in perfect condition except one of the magi was missing. The farmer's son had a little run-in with the visiting royalty on his return from a New Year's Eve party. Not to worry; Anton had the problem of the absent magi all figured out. They set up a dozen straw bales in a kind of amphitheater shape. He instructed Lyle to set all the characters except for one camel in front of the bales. "Hide the last camel behind the bales with just his hind quarters sticking out. That way," Anton said, "if anyone asks where the other wise man is, just tell him he's out back getting his gift ready." On this Friday, Anton was headed out to see what kind of a job Lyle was doing setting it up.

Lyle is about as easygoing as any man could be. He's a slender man, about five feet ten, with no remarkable characteristics except for his pipe and his bib overalls. And given the places that Lyle frequents, even those were not particularly remarkable. There is one other thing, but it's so much a part of Lyle hardly anyone notices it. Lyle has a little bit of a limp. That's how Lyle got the job as church custodian in the first place.

Lyle was born with this kind of twisted foot. I suppose today they would have done surgery to straighten it out, but around Pleasant View in 1946, people accepted their condition at birth as a kind of divine mandate. For the most part, people didn't say much about Lyle's foot. With so few people around, they really didn't have the luxury of putting anybody on disability. So Lyle did all the same chores his brothers and sisters did. He chased the cows home when it was time to milk and climbed up in the haymow when it was time to feed them. It was pretty much the same at school. They just accepted that Lyle wasn't as fast on his feet as some kids, so when they played softball, Lyle was the catcher. When they played football, he was the center. And when the youth did the worship service, they made Lyle the preacher because Lyle didn't like to talk much and that made his sermons a more digestible length than Pastor Jacobson's were.

Things went along fine until 1965 when Lyle got his draft notice. He reported to Rapid City for his physical. Lyle wasn't the brightest guy in Pleasant View, but he certainly had never flunked a test, at least, not until that day. Lyle saw the doctor scribble a note next to his name, "Unfit to serve per physical defect." Two weeks later, Lyle got a letter in the mail. He was classified "IV-F, registrant not qualified for any military service." Lyle was shocked. He simply had never considered before that someone could be "unfit to serve." But seeing it there in black and white, written by a man in a uniform, made it seem so true that he simply could not argue with it. You might as well have written it on his forehead.

That weekend, Lyle talked his dad into moving the dairy herd to the north eighty. He moved into the old homestead there and became a kind of recluse. It took the people of Pleasant View about three months to figure out what was going on, and then it took them another three months to get up the courage to go and talk to him. Lars Oland drew the short straw and showed up on Lyle's step. He told Lyle the church needed a janitor, and they all thought he was the guy to do it. Lyle didn't want the job. People at Pleasant View can smell sympathy from a mile away, and this request reeked of pity. But it was harder to say no than to argue, so he said yes.

Lyle took his sentence in stride. Pretty soon he was back at church, making sure the place looked presentable and the front door was unlocked. Lyle became an expert at keeping the old boiler running. He spent a good many Saturday nights sitting up with it just like he was nursing one of his sick calves. He listened to the clanking of the pipes like a doctor listening to the beating of an old patient's heart. That's when he stared to smoke a pipe.

Something to keep him awake during those long nights. At a quarter to eight, he put on the coffeepot.

People came in on a Sunday morning, smelled that mix of Norwegian coffee, pipe tobacco, and fuel oil, and knew everything was going to be just fine. Lyle would slip into the furnace room, change out of his bibs and flannels into his black slacks and white cowboy shirt, and become a one-man greeting committee. Every floor was buffed, every carpet swept, every piece of old oak polished with love, and every piece of glass made squeaky clean. Lyle always had a joke in his pocket and a smile on his face. He opened the door for you like he was welcoming you into his home, and I guess in some ways, that's exactly what he was doing.

On this particular Friday, Lyle wore a gold pin on one of the straps of his bibs. It had an engraving of a set of church doors, swung wide open, with the reference Psalm 84:10 stamped across the bottom. Pastor Loeson gave it to Lyle on the occasion of his thirtieth anniversary as church janitor. The pastor was looking through some old church council minutes, trying to settle an argument between Mable Trogemann and Marguerite Oland about some gravy boats (believe me, you don't want to hear about it) when he came across Lyle's appointment as church custodian. What struck him was that Lyle had been appointed thirty years ago nearly to the day. He decided there should be some kind of reward for that kind of service, so the two of them drove down to Sioux Falls for an all-day seminar on volunteerism and a steak dinner at the Cattleman's Club. The pin was one of about fifty different pins used to honor volunteers. The one with the doors on it was really for ushers, but Lyle didn't seem to mind. He quoted the verse referenced on it, "I'd rather be a doorkeeper in the house of the Lord than dwell in the tents of the wicked."

Anton pulled in the yard just as Lyle was picking up the plastic, soon to be illuminated Jesus. He pulled out a faded blue bandanna, and like a mother washing her newborn, Lyle began to dust the dirt off the Christ Child. Anton asked him about his trip with the pastor. "It was all right," he said. "I know it sounds kinda stupid, but back when I was in high school doing those youth services, I used to think about becoming a pastor. I used to get into the pulpit and think how important it was to serve God. I'd get so scared and shaky that I'd actually pray, 'Lord, I just want to be your servant. Help me keep my head on my shoulders and my foot out of my mouth.' But then I went and took that physical and got that letter from the draft board. IV-F, it said. 'Unfit to serve,' that doctor said. I said to myself, 'Lyle, who are you kidding. You ain't never gonna be no preacher. You ain't never gonna be nothing.'"

Lyle rolled the baby Jesus over and scraped away at a smudge on the baby's backside. "They made me take this job as a janitor, and at first, I hated it. But slowly, I got used to it. At least I wasn't out in the barn. And people depended on me. When the furnace wasn't working, they called me. When they wanted everything to look just right, they called me. The day Maxine Halverson died, her family came out to the church, and I served them coffee and talked to them until the pastor got here. You know what; they sent me a card that said, 'Thank you for your ministry during our time of grief.' Before that, no one ever called what I was doing a ministry.

"When the pastor and I were down in Sioux Falls, you were supposed to go to these classes. They were serving coffee at one of the sessions, so I went in there. There was a young woman in there talking about gifts. She gave us a sheet of paper and told us to write down all our gifts. You know, I couldn't think of a single gift to write down. I kept looking at that sheet of paper, and all I could see was *IV-F, Unfit to Serve*. This other woman was helping people out. She come up to me and says, 'Why don't you have anything written on your paper?' I said, 'Well, I guess I'm just not a very gifted guy.'

"So she starts asking me all kinds of questions about what I do at church and on my farm and everything. 'Who polishes that brass?' she asks and 'Who keeps that furnace going?' and 'Who sat with those cows when they're calving?' and all kinds of questions like that. Pretty soon I've got my paper full. She takes my paper and looks at my name tag and she writes across the top of my paper, in big letters, 'Lyle Hegland, Servant of God.'

"I just sat there staring at that paper and I thought about how long I'd been carrying around that letter IV-F on my head. That woman must have known what I was thinking so she says really soft, 'You know what, Lyle? You really are a gifted person. Look at all the things you know how to do. And with all that talent that God has given you, you are God's gift to everyone you meet. I'll tell you something else. Lyle Hegland may be the greatest Christmas gift Pleasant View Lutheran Church gets this year.' Then she goes off to harass some other poor guy with nothing on his paper."

Lyle stuck the big bandanna back in his pocket. He knelt down and put the baby in the manger and plugged it in. He fluffed up the straw around it like he was fixing a bed for a real newborn. He picked up the Christ Child, and he looked at it while he continued to talk to Anton.

"I wonder if Jesus knew that he was God's gift to everyone he met. I mean, look at him. Here he is, born in this stable to this poor carpenter and this frightened little girl. He goes through life teaching people what they need to be taught, healing people the way they need to be healed, and making them know that they are important to God. And when it's all said and done, what happens to him? All the religious people are mad at him. His disciples run away from him. And the Romans, they nail him to a cross. He ends up spending his life loving the world. His whole life was God's gift to the world.

"I sure never thought of myself as God's gift."

Lyle laid down the Christ Child and asked Anton to watch while he went in and turned on the power. Anton watched Lyle walk away and thought about Lyle carrying around that piece of paper that said IV-F, Unfit to Serve. He wondered how many people carry around a piece of paper like that. He knew he sure had. He thought about all those people trying to do everything they could to prove that little piece of paper wrong. Some try to bury it beneath a pile of money or a closet full of expensive clothes. Some try to hide it behind rippling muscles or military might or political prowess.

Anton looked at the infant in the manger. If the pastor would have asked him, he could have written his Christmas sermon for him. "Look at this little baby here. Born as a gift. He takes our rejection notices and tears them up. He takes the scathing little letters that others send us or that we write to ourselves. He takes all them all and writes across the top "Servant of God" in letters that are big enough and bold enough that not even our insecure spirits can argue with the proclamation. Christmas is the time of the year when we remember that God sends us the gift of a son who reminds us of our own giftedness."

Lyle turned on the power, and the whole Nativity scene lit up, even the back end of the camel that was hiding behind the stable, waiting for the magi to get his gift ready. It kind of makes sense to have the camel there. It's a gentle reminder to all of us that we need to get our gifts ready as well. It's a gentle reminder of the magnificent gift that was given us and how that gift calls us to be prepared to give ourselves away as well.

Lyle came back and the scene met with his approval. He said good-bye to Anton and excused himself to go down and get the rest of the Christmas decorations out. Anton got into his car and watched Lyle limp back into the church and thought to himself, *There goes Lyle Hegland, servant of God, gift of God to everyone he meets.*

Red Johnson:
Carpenter Extraordinaire

December 25, 1996

Red Johnson was good with his hands.

When he as a kid, he disappeared for an afternoon, and his mom nearly went crazy looking for him. She finally found him on the north eighty, clear on the other side of the section. He was out behind the old alleyway, playing with some baling wire and corncobs. By the time she got there, he had created an entire old-west city complete with livery stable, dance hall, and salon. He made a little mud figure of himself, a horse, and a buxom little dance-hall girl. The two of them were set to ride off into the sunset when his mother discovered him. She was somewhat less than impressed. Red was fast on his feet even as a child, so he quickly asked her if she'd like to help him build a chapel. What could she say?

When he got a little older, his grandpa took him under his wing and introduced him to woodworking. Red was a natural. From his first footstool to the grandfather's clock he built for his dad, he just had a way with wood. His grandfather used to say that Red could mold wood in his hands like most people mold clay. He ran his fingers over the wood like it was an old friend. His blades caressed the backs of hutches until oak leaves and acorns look liked they had grown right there in the middle of the plank. Red could turn his mother's sweetest dreams into polished oak in the space of a week once the idea got into his head and the will got into his heart.

Red's greatest gift was his knack for detail. He once made a set of clocks for his three sisters. All three were identical, made of cherry wood with German works he ordered from the Amish down in Iowa. As a gag, he took the clocks all apart and threw the pieces into one big box and had the women open it. The pieces were so finely turned and the finish so perfectly matched that they could pick any combination of pieces they wanted and he could assemble them into a clock.

But his greatest strength was also his weakness. Red had no patience for imperfection. Red always said, "If it ain't worth doing right, it just ain't worth doing." Once he burned an entire load of oak in his fireplace because he found out the sawyer had rushed the curing by stacking the wood around the potbellied stove in his machine shed. He took an order for a footstool, and before he was done, he had half a dozen imperfect footstools lying out in the scrap pile behind his shop. He took an order for a hope chest for a girl when she was fourteen and didn't have it ready until the day before she was married on her eighteenth birthday.

Red was his own worst enemy. He was always friendly with everybody he met, but you didn't want to be around him when he worked. He would call himself every name in the book. In his mind, if it wasn't perfect, it was worthless, and worthless work could only be made by a worthless man.

Well, in spite of Red's low opinion of himself, the good people of Pleasant View Lutheran Church loved his work. And his greatest patron was Marguerite Oland, the chair of the Christian Martyrs Circle. That's why when Marguerite accidentally collapsed the church's manger by sitting on it, Red's name was the first thing that came out of her mouth. (Well, actually, it was the second thing that came out of her mouth. I won't repeat the first thing that came out of her mouth.)

Let me start at the beginning. It all happened last July when Marguerite was snooping around the church's belfry. She found a 1948 membership giving report listing the contributions of every member of Pleasant View. It would make for a good read. She went to sit down on what looked like an old apple crate covered with a sheet and had a rude awakening. Now maybe that old manger had the strength to hold the savior of the universe, but it didn't have the architectural fortitude to hold over two hundred pounds of aging Christian flesh. After Marguerite picked herself up off the floor, she picked up the shattered pieces of manger, threw them all in the old sheet and snuck over to Red Johnston's place.

I'm not sure what Marguerite told Red but before she left, she talked him into not only making a new manger but also carving an infant Christ Child that would fit perfectly into Marguerite's christening outfit. She swore Red into the deepest secrecy so that the newly clothed Christ and his manger would be what she called "a delightful surprise" at the Christmas Eve worship service.

Marguerite had no idea of the kind of torment the assignment caused Red. She would have asked him anyway even if she did know. It's just that, in this case, her innocence was purely accidental. As soon as Marguerite left, Red knew he made a mistake. He ran back out into the yard, tried to catch her, but Marguerite couldn't—or more likely wouldn't—hear his calls. One of Marguerite's greatest virtues in life was the inability to hear the word *no*.

Red went back inside and slumped down in the old metal lawn chair he kept by the lathe. It was hard enough for Red when he worked on a project for his neighbors at Pleasant View. It was even worse when he was asked to do a project for the church. Maybe he could have even handled making a new manger. But to form the Son of God with his own hand, that was simply too much. He shook his head and cursed himself for being so stupid.

In the months that followed, Red grew more and more ill at ease. It took him two months just to pick out the right kind of wood. He bought a wagon load of white pine and then spent the next month just looking through it, trying to find clear pieces of pine without blemish. He started the project a hundred times. He finally managed to complete the manger, but he couldn't make any headway on the Christ Child. After only minutes of work, the imperfection of his hands would taint the perfect child and he would have to start all over again. The scrap pile behind the shop grew to enormous proportions.

Things went on like that right up until a week before Christmas. Thursday afternoon, Red was watching his nephew for his sister. Nathan sat on the floor and played with some scraps of wood and a tack hammer Red gave him. Red was bent over the bench. Spread before him were a half dozen art books, a picture

Bible and his sister's baby album. Red pored over the pictures, trying to grasp something that would give him some inspiration.

Nathan dropped the hammer and walked over to his uncle. "Whatcha doing, Uncle Red?"

"Looking at some pictures."

"Why ya doing that?"

Red said, "I've got to make something, and I want to know what it looks like."

"Can I see?"

Red picked up Nathan and held him on his lap. Nathan turned the pages of the book and looked at the pictures. "Do you know what that is?"

"That's the baby Jesus and that's his Mom and that's his Dad. That's the stable Jesus was born in. Are you gonna build a stable, Uncle Red?" Nathan asked.

"Nope. I wish it were that easy. I've got to build—I mean, make one of these." He pointed to the baby.

"Okay," Nathan said and slid down from his uncle's lap. Red went back to looking at the books. Nathan walked around the shop and stopped by a wooden box in the corner. "Hey, Uncle Red, what's this stuff?"

Red looked up for a minute and then looked back down, talking from the pages of the book. "That's some dirt your Aunt Sylvia was gonna use to repot her plants, but it's got too much clay in it."

"Can I play in it?"

Red was impatient, "Listen, Nathan, your Uncle Red's got work to do. Can you just play by yourself?"

"Okay, Uncle Red."

Red could feel the pressure building up in his chest. He only had a week. But he knew it really didn't matter if he had a week or a month or even a year. He just couldn't do it. He closed the book and stared down at his calloused and dirty hands. How could he have been so stupid as to accept this assignment? What does the Son of God have to do with such worthless human flesh?

Red remembered a day long ago, standing next to his grandfather in his shop. His grandfather was trying to fix a clock that one of his neighbors brought in. A fly-by-night salesman sold it to his neighbor. It worked for exactly eight days and then fell apart. His grandfather was mad and said, "Look at this mess, Red. It's nothing but junk. Just a pile of dirt. And the guys that built it, they're just a pile of dirt too. And that man that sold it to Emil and then left town, he's the worst of all. Just a great big pile of dirt."

That's how Red felt. He looked over at his most recent attempt at the Christ Child and said to himself, "Just a big pile of dirt. And the man that made it, an even bigger pile of dirt. What can God do with a pile of dirt?"

Red shook his head, and then he felt someone pulling on the leg of his bib overalls. It was Nathan.

"Uncle Red, I got a present for you! Come and see!"

Red got up and walked over to the box of dirt. Nathan bent down and scooped up his earthen gift and handed it Red. It looked like a doll made out of dirt.

"What's this?" Red said.

"It's the baby Jesus," Nathan said. "I made him just for you."

"Out of dirt?"

"Yeah, Mrs. Eller told me that God made a man out of dirt. She said that God made all of us, and that we're really important to God. So I made a baby Jesus just for you out of dirt. Merry Christmas, Uncle Red."

Red didn't know whether to laugh or cry. A baby Jesus made out of dirt. A baby Jesus made with loving hands just the way God stooped down in the dirt and made the first human being. Nathan had no idea what a special gift he had given Red. Red held it lovingly in his hands, dirt to dirt.

"Well, do you like it? Nathan said.

"Yes, I do, Nathan. Yes, I do, very much indeed."

On Christmas Eve, the church was packed. Pastor Loeson handed Red the only key to the big cabinet behind the sacristy and then went to get dressed. Marguerite was seated in the first pew, right on the aisle, so she could drink in the glory of the baby Jesus appearing clad in her christening outfit. The lights were turned down low and mystery descended on the little white-framed church like some kind of holy perfume. The children sang, and little boys magically became shepherds and kings. Little girls stood up in the front, with golden garlands in their hair, and suddenly, the room was filed with the beautiful voices of angels. Mary and Joseph found their way into the stable, and holiness filled the room.

Pastor Loeson and Red walked silently out of the sacristy, carrying the manger and the Christ Child. The manger was more beautiful than any manger that had ever been seen. It was solid, rough-hewn oak on the outside and beautiful, finely rubbed walnut on the inside. The Christ Child lay securely in a pure white christening dress. Marguerite and all the rest strained their eyes and craned their necks to see the baby, but his face was hidden by the dancing shadows of the candles. But that was okay. In their own hearts, they knew exactly what the child looked like. Faith had already drawn the picture there with indelible ink.

Pastor Loeson stepped into the pulpit and said, "Being human is a very strange thing to be. On the one hand, there is nothing more beautiful than a newborn child—perfectly formed little rose-colored fingernails, eyelashes as delicate as lace, silky hair, and that new-baby smell. On the other hand, there is perhaps nothing so repulsive as a human gone wrong. A face twisted in jealousy, hands clenched in greed, a heart cold with hatred, lips curled in a snarl of defiance. Sometimes the beauty of our creatureliness is so great we could almost weep. Sometimes the deathly odor of our sin is so vile it makes us retch. It's a strange thing to be a human.

"But it is stranger still that God would choose to take on human flesh, with all its beauty and all its propensity for corruption. And yet on this day, that is what we celebrate. Long ago, God knelt in the muck and formed the first human being. Thousands of years later, God picked up the mud again, made himself into a human being and came and dwelt among us.

"Because God chose to descend into the dirt, to take on flesh, we dare to live in hope. We know that all of us are made of frail human flesh, nothing more than mud in the shape of humanity. And yet because God climbed into a muddy form like ours, we know we can be redeemed. We know we can be made beautiful again. We know that we can dare to live as people made and remade by the loving hand of God."

The congregation all nodded in agreement. After the service, they went downstairs and drank their coffee and ate their cookies. No one saw Marguerite sneak back upstairs to the sanctuary. None of them heard her turn on the lights and creep over to the Christ Child in his manger. None of them heard her gasp as she saw laid there, in her sacred family christening gown, the Christ Child—lovingly formed out of mud. And certainly, none of them saw the curious look on her face when she saw a little earthen carpenter doll wearing blue bib overalls held firmly in the arms of the Christ Child. Marguerite just shook her head, stumbled out of the sanctuary and drove home. Downstairs, Red Johnston, carpenter extraordinaire and a redeemed child of God, whistled a soundless version of "Silent Night" as he smiled and drank another cup of coffee.

Betty and Frank Olson:
The Sacred and the Profane
December 25, 1997

I
t's been a good year for Pastor Michael Loeson. Every year in January, Luther Seminary graduates from all over the country gather in St. Paul for Convocation. This year, Pastor Loeson was asked to be a presenter for one of the small groups. Pastor Loeson is pretty excited about it. His topic has to do with Christmas as a theological intersection between the sacred and the profane and its implication for daily ministry. His paper was due right after Christmas, so, to take some of the pressure off, Michael enlisted the help of Betty Olson, the church secretary, as a copy editor.

Betty Olson was not having a good year.

It all started when she attended the Scandinavian smorgasbord down at East Nidaros Lutheran Church just outside of Baltic. While she was waiting to get into the smorgasbord, she discovered one of those Christian romance novels lying in one of the pews. Before she got to page twelve, she was hooked. It was the story of a handsome young Christian bookseller named Dirk and his beautiful wife, Tiffany. The book was full of candlelight, fervent prayers, and more than enough trembling hearts to keep the attention of any good Christian woman.

Betty was especially susceptible to this kind of literature because of the way things were at home. You may remember that she and her husband, Frank, were farmers. They also raised donkeys for the donkey basketball circuit. Frank was a loving, compassionate man. That's why Betty married him. But you see, Frank was not a particularly romantic man. He was about as emotive as one of those guards you see standing in front of Buckingham Palace. She heard a joke, one that pretty well summed up Frank's romantic propensities.

> After forty years of marriage, Lena found herself living on a starvation diet of affection. Ole never expressed his love for her. Finally, Lena could stand it no longer.
>
> "Ole," she asked, "why don't you ever tell me that you love me?"
>
> Ole gave her a puzzled look and replied, Lena, forty years ago, on the day we were married, I told you I loved you. If I ever change my mind, I'll let you know."

Now in the Christian romance novel, Dirk was a walking ball of passion. He was always surprising Tiffany with romantic weekends in Paris and love notes hidden away in her Holy Word

Attaché Case. It seems that every time they got together, Dirk was passionately confessing his love to Tiffany. He was religiously romantic. Frank, on the other hand, was about as erotic as chipped beef on toast.

It all came to a head on Betty's birthday just a week ago. Betty took Frank down to Sioux Falls and led him to the door of one of those intimate-apparel shops. She shoved him into the store and told him not to come out until he had a birthday gift for her. Frank performed a miracle. Somewhere in that store, Frank found a lovely pair of red wool hiking socks. What had been a mild winter at the Olson home quickly came to an end with the hard frost that set in when Betty opened the present.

The only redeeming feature of the whole season was that Betty's favorite niece, Carolyn, her husband, John, and their newborn son were selected to play the role of the Holy Family for the living Nativity at Pleasant View. Their son was adorable, the perfect Christ Child. She was certain that at least they would represent the true meaning of Christmas.

Unaware of Betty's newfound love for the Christian romance genre, Pastor Loeson gave Betty his paper to proofread. When he got it back, he was more than a little surprised with some of the rewriting that Betty did. The language was a little bit more purple than he was comfortable with. Some of the writing in the sacred sections even left him a little breathless. But he admitted that the paper could use a little punching up and page by page, they negotiated a pretty good document.

The final negotiation took place at noon on Christmas Eve. It involved the title. Pastor Loeson wanted to call his paper "The Interface of the Secular and the Profane in the Incarnation: Implications for Ministry." Betty's title included both the word *love* and something about intertwining and Pastor Loeson was less than comfortable with that. They settled on the title "Christmas, Where God and Humanity Dance: A Call to Caring Relationships." With great pride, Pastor Loeson laid the completed manuscript on his desk.

Betty went home, got dressed, got the kids ready, and then went over to her niece's house to help get her ready. Frank said he'd meet her at the church after chores. By six thirty, Betty and her niece's family were all at the church, ready for the dress rehearsal.

Betty sat alone in the pew as the pastor turned down the lights. The Holy Family took their places. To set the mood, the organ softly played "Infant Holy, Infant Lowly" in the background. Betty watched in awe. No matter how many times she saw it, this scene took her breath away. It was so sacred, so holy, and so perfect. Soft light fell on the holy virgin's face. Her husband looked on with holy adoration. The child cooed softly as his beautiful eyes moved back and forth between his admiring parents. The organ played the phrase, "Christ the babe is lord of all." The perfect child. The perfect moment. The perfect harmony. An air of peace and tranquility filled the sanctuary. For a moment, Betty drifted off into deep thought. This is what Christmas is about. The world is as it should be: beautiful, warm, romantic, and perfect.

But suddenly, Carolyn's cry broke the silence. "Oh, for Christ's sake!" she yelled. "Kevin just peed all over me. John, didn't I tell you to put a fresh diaper on him? Man, look at this. The swaddling clothes are soaked. Look at my gown. It's ruined. What are we supposed to do now?"

This sudden intrusion of reality into the holy scene put Betty into a kind of incarnational shock. She had been floating in a sacred bliss and wasn't quite ready for the profane. It wasn't until the pastor flipped on the lights that she was able to come to her senses. She ran up to the front of the church and picked up the Christ Child. When she realized just how wet he really was, she held him at arm's length and carried him toward the church office. She yelled over her shoulder, "Carolyn, you go get cleaned up," "There's another costume down in the nursery. I'll take care of little Jesus here."

Now even at his very best, Frank was not known for his timing. When Betty burst into the office, there sat Frank, casually sitting at the pastor's desk, reading the pastor's paper. The soaking Christ Child and her less-than-romantic husband was more reality than Betty was prepared to deal with. "Here," she scolded, as if Frank were in cahoots with whatever profane power had caused the Christ Child to wet himself. "Change this child. I'm going to find something to wrap him in."

Frank obediently took the child and Betty climbed up on a stool, opening and slamming cupboard doors as she looked for something to wrap the infant in. Her frustration grew with every door she opened. Where was Ruby's tablecloth? Finally, she could take it no longer. She plopped down on the counter top and started to silently sob.

Through her tears, Betty watched Frank's back as he helplessly looked around for a place to change the soaking Christ Child. There he was—Mr. Routine, Mr. Mundane, mediocrity incarnate—holding in his hands the salvation of the world. She wanted to point and say, "You see, this is what I'm talking about. You wouldn't even know it if the savior of the universe fell into your hands."

But she didn't. She just watched, and as she watched, her anger began to soften. She had watched him hold their babies that same way a thousand times. And she had to admit, he was a natural at caring. His head leaned ever so slightly in the direction of the crying baby as he whispered, "Shush, shush. We can fix this." His hands holding firmly and yet gently touching. It was the same gentle touch, the same quiet tone he used when he walked up behind the donkeys and laid his big hand on their rumps and whispered, "How you doing, girl?"

Frank walked over to the pastor's desk and laid the baby right on top of the pastor's paper. Betty took a breath to warn him, but it was too late. She just watched as Frank went about his task, oblivious to the incongruity of it all. The loftiest of Pastor Loeson's scholarly work soaked with the musky earthiness of a baby's wet diaper. The Son of God, the King of the universe, touched by a farmer's hand with the same familiarity he used to soothe his donkeys.

As she watched what should have been an offence, she felt herself somehow quietly calmed. It all seemed so right. It was as though part of the magnificence of this Christ Child was his ordinariness. It was as though his magnificence in some way blessed the ordinary. The sacredness of God wrapped up in the profanity of a crying baby with wet diapers. It was as though one could honor this king just as well with a diaper change as one could honor him with gold, frankincense, and myrrh.

Frank finished his job and wrapped the baby up in a little receiving blanket. Betty looked at Frank and remembered why she loved him. It wasn't because of his great propensity for romantic fantasy. It wasn't for his amorous surprises. She loved him for his consistency. Every day, he was there for her. Every day, she knew what to expect. Every day, he supported her and loved her. There was no great drama in it, only security. His care was a kind of unplanned, meditated, unconditional love. There was a kind of godly grace in the everydayness of it.

She walked up behind him and slid her arms around him, laying her cheek against his back, squeezing him into a hug. Frank cooed. "Now that's about the nicest Christmas gift a guy could get." He picked up the baby and turned to give her a big kiss on the forehead, sliding the baby into her arms. Together, they turned back to the desk to assess the damage. Betty looked down and laughed at the soaked papers. "It looks like Pastor's sacred writings have had an encounter with the profane," Betty laughed. Frank laughed too.

While they both looked at the mess Frank began to speak. "Betty, I'm sorry. I've been reading the pastor's paper. He talks about Christ as a gift to the world that changes everything. He says that the entire world was created to be sacred but that our sinfulness made it all profane. Sin shattered the unity of the universe. A dark line was drawn between the sacred and the profane. Christ came to break down that barrier. To shatter those things falsely called sacred. To redeem those things proclaimed profane. He says that because God took on earthly flesh in the person of Jesus Christ, even the most everyday action can become a sacred thing. He says that everything we have—our jobs, ourselves, our relationship—can become sacred things because of the birth of this child.

"I'm not sure how, but somewhere along the way, I have failed to recognize just how sacred our relationship is. I remember when my father gave me his father's watch. He told me it would last a very long time if I took care of it. He told me to value it so that I could pass it on to my children. I've done that. I have watched over that watch like it was a precious child. But I have not always watched over our relationship like that. I just take it for granted that you'll always be there. I'm sorry. You deserve better than that. I want to change. I want you to know that even when I don't tell you so, you are special to me. I intend for things to be different in the future. I think I owe you that much. I think I owe God that much."

Betty about melted. The Christian bookseller, Dirk, had never said anything so beautiful. She thought, *Maybe being married to just a plain old farmer isn't such a bad thing after all.*

Just then, Carolyn walked in. She looked a little worse for wear, but probably looked a lot better than how Mary looked on that first night that the sacred burst into the profane. She took the baby, went, and hid out in the sacristy until it was their time to come out. Frank and Betty took their place in the pew and watched the story they had seen dozens of times one more time, but this time, they did it holding hands.

In January, Pastor Loeson gave his paper. It was well received even if some of the language was a bit flowery. But the paper had a far greater effect on Betty and Frank than it did on any of those pastors. I'd like to tell you that Frank took Betty on a Caribbean cruise, but he didn't. They did make it down to Saint Louis to see the arch. And Betty did talk Frank into dancing with her until the band put their instruments away. And perhaps more important still, they both came to realize that there is something sacred about everyday love. That the mundane, everyday things we do to care for one another are important. That God dared to take on flesh because it is in those everyday, flesh-to-flesh relationships that most of us really come to know grace. That the care of our brothers and sisters, husbands and wives, children and parents is holy work. It is part of the dance that God started at Christmas when he sent his son to dwell among us. Betty still has a stack of those Christian romance novels, but she doesn't read them much anymore. Every once in a while, she'll pull one out and ask Frank to read to her. He always complains, but in the end, he always gives in. "After all," Betty giggles, "it is sacred work."

Marguerite Oland:
The Receiving Blanket

December 25, 1998

This fall has been difficult for Marguerite Oland. You may remember Marguerite. Folks at Pleasant View have a saying about her: "Pastors come and pastors go, but we all know who runs the show." Generally, Marguerite is able to run a tight ship, but occasionally there are challenges even in a small parish like Pleasant View, and this fall has been one challenge after another.

It started back in September when she was down with the flu for nearly a month—the same month that the Christian Martyrs Circle had its annual election. Marguerite has been the chair of the Christian Martyrs Circle as long as there has been a Christian Martyrs Circle. Generally, nothing happens in that circle without her okay, but in some kind of Indian-summer delirium, the circle decided to have an election without her. And somehow—no one remembers how exactly—the circle ended up electing Ellen White as its chair. Ellen is a newcomer to the parish. She moved into a local retirement apartment just after her husband died in July. Being a newcomer and all, she didn't know it was impolite to allow yourself to be elected the chair of Marguerite's circle. Marguerite was enraged, but with Ellen being a widow and all, she said she felt like she couldn't say a word. And it must be true because there are a dozen or more people who say she told them that.

The second blow came when Marguerite's Holiday Ham Loaf was preempted as the entrée for the congregational Christmas dinner. For nearly twenty years, the Christian Martyrs Circle has hosted the dinner, and for nearly half of those twenty years, they served Marguerite's Holiday Ham Loaf. To be fair, these loaves really were something to see. They were baked in the shape of a wreath, with hotdog slices randomly placed like holly berries in each seasonal ring. Their crowning glories were pineapple slices trimmed and reconstructed into golden bows with pineapple leaves winging their way out on either side. The Christian Martyrs women marched in solemn procession in black skirts, red blouses, and green vests to lovingly deck the hall with swinely elegance. But the glory of the ham loaves met its untimely demise when Anton Anderson's prized turkeys got out of the pen about a week before the dinner. It was midnight, and at an inopportune moment, the turkeys flapped their way onto Anton's lane. At the same inopportune moment, Anton was coming home from the Scandinavian service club meeting in town where, ironically, the spirit du jour was nothing less than Santa Beer with a Wild Turkey chaser. Anton veered to miss the newly liberated birds.

When the frozen dust cleared, there sat Anton's brand new Chrysler, smashed against his concrete silage bunker. The next morning, Anton got a good look at the damage to his Chrysler and he suddenly didn't prize his turkeys nearly as much as he used to. The Christian Martyrs Circle ended up with about 150 pounds of turkey, and Marguerite was informed that they wouldn't need her holiday loaf this year.

The final blow came when Marguerite won the right to deliver the Christmas cookie boxes to the homebound. Each member drew a yuletide ministry from the Joyful Service cookie jar. Marguerite really had her heart set on doing the inspirational reading at the Christmas party. She had already gathered thirty-five moving sayings out of the greeting cards she had collected over the years. She mentioned her disappointment to the group when she failed to draw the inspirational reading ministry card from the jar, but no one insisted on trading with her (which would have been the polite thing to do). She felt like no one appreciated her talent. They didn't want her as chair of the circle. They didn't want her ham loaf. Now, they didn't want her incarnational musings. In short, she decided, they didn't want her.

Dejected but not defeated, Marguerite decided it was about time someone added both efficiency and inspiration to the task of cookie delivery. First, she chopped her Hallmarkian incarnation presentation into twelve equal parts and taped three pithy statements onto each cookie box. Next, she mapped the course she would take to deliver the goodies. Finally, she wrote a brief poem she would recite to disentangle herself from any interpersonal distractions her visit-starved, time-sucking home bounders might throw at her.

I truly wish that I could stay
To cheer your world, perhaps to pray
But God bids me be on my way
I have a dozen smiles to share today.

She loaded up the car and clicked through the stops. By 1:00 p.m., she had delivered six of the twelve holiday boxes and thought she needed a break. She caught the Tannenbaum Tuna Melt Special at the Bungalow and allowed herself to be dragged into a little too much gossip. By the time she shared all she knew, it was two thirty, and she still had six boxes to deliver all over the county. In a blur, she raced down the back alley to Ingeborg Lutsen's place.

Ingeborg Lutsen was about the sweetest old saint you'd ever hope to meet. She lived in an old two-story farmhouse that was moved into town when her son built his new place on the home forty. As the years went by, her arthritis caught up with her. First, she became homebound. Then the kids limited her to the first floor. Now, she pretty much lives in what she calls the front room. But she doesn't let it get her down. Her hands look like the gnarled roots of the old cedar tree in the backyard, but they are always busy. She has thick old-fashioned cataract glasses and always keeps at least two crochet hooks stuck in the bun at the back of her head. He son gave her a bright light with a magnifying glass in it so she can still do her "fancy work" of crocheting, needlepoint, and embroidery. There is hardly a home in Pleasant View that doesn't have at least one piece of Ingeborg's work in it somewhere. From afghans to trim for wedding dresses, she does it all. She was the one who crocheted the lace abound Ruby Green's tablecloth when they decided to use it as the altar cloth for Christmas Communion. She's a countywide legend, but you'd never know it to see her sitting bug-eyed and bent over in her automatic lift chair in the front room of her drafty house.

Marguerite rushed to her front door and read the note under the black button there. "Push it once and wait. I move slow." Marguerite pushed the button. A buzzer sounded and Ingeborg intoned a melodic "I'm coming." Marguerite drummed her fingers on the cookie box impatiently. She could see the ritual taking place in the front room. Ingeborg moved more slowly than a parishioner on the way to a stewardship interview. First she stuck the crochet hook in her hair for safekeeping. Then she carefully folded the afghan she had been working on. Painfully, she pulled her walker into position. She fumbled with the remote on her lift chair. In slow motion, the chair raised her to a standing position, and Ingeborg stopped there for a full minute, stilling her spinning head. The she fumbled with the remote switch that returned the chair to its seated position. Secure that the chair was in place, she straightened her hair and tugged her sweater into place.

"Good Lord!" Marguerite muttered to herself and grabbed the porch door to let herself in. When it wouldn't budge, she rattled it, hoping to shake it loose but no such luck. Ingeborg heard the rattle and called out with the same maddening cheerfulness, "I'm on my way." Marguerite watched as Ingeborg made what seemed to be a three-day journey across the front room to the front door. Then she watched as Ingeborg took another three days to reach up and get the key to the door that hung near the top of the doorframe. Time stood still as Ingeborg struggled to unlock the door. Another millennium passed as Ingeborg crossed the porch to unhook the porch door.

Marguerite forced herself to paste a paper smile on her face and shoved the box of cookies into Ingeborg's hand's, said "Merry

Christmas from the Christian Martyrs," and then, with an air of solemnity, "And always remember, 'Jesus is the reason for the season.'" With that, she turned to leave.

But Ingeborg called out, "Thank you so much. Won't you come in? I've got something for you."

Marguerite started, "*I truly wish that I could stay, to cheer your world, perhaps to pray . . .*" But in her elevated state of frustration, she forgot the rest. No Christian woman could repeat the other words that swirled in her head.

"Oh, everybody's got time for coffee with a friend," Ingeborg said. "Besides, it won't take long. The coffee's already perked, and I've got the rosettes on a plate. I won't take no for an answer." And with that, Ingeborg turned and headed for the front room. Marguerite considered pretending not to hear and going on her way, but Ingeborg turned around and looked at her through those bug eyes, and not even Marguerite could say no. She waited for Ingeborg to pass through the door and followed her into the front room. She took off her scarf and coat and threw them on the sofa. The perking coffeepot, two cups, and a plate full of rosettes sat on a TV tray next to Ingeborg's chair. Ingeborg directed Marguerite to an ancient overstuffed chair bathed in the midafternoon sunlight.

They ate their rosettes and drank their coffee and Marguerite did the polite thing and asked Ingeborg about her Christmas plans, even though on the day before Christmas Eve, everybody already knows everybody's Christmas plans along with the plans of most of their relatives. Marguerite felt her eyes grow heavy as the warm sunlight, the rosettes, and Ingeborg's gentle voice did their work. The last thing Marguerite heard was Ingeborg climbing up into the third bough of the family tree as she traced the lineage of the Olson girl that the one-armed brother named Oscar married in 1948.

Marguerite was awakened by the ringing of the phone and Ingeborg's whispered responses. Ingeborg hung up the phone and said, "Well, did you have a nice little nap then, Marguerite? That used to be my favorite chair too for taking a little snooze after lunch."

Marguerite was mortified. She started to apologize, but Ingeborg shushed her and reached for a package sitting on footstool by her chair. She looked at the package as she made her explanation. "Every year, for as long as I can remember, there's been a baby in my life. First it was my little brothers and sisters. Then it was my nieces and nephews. Finally, it was my own children and grandchildren and great-grandchildren and their nieces and nephews and cousins. So every year, I just start on one of these things, and sure enough, by the time I finish it, another baby comes along. But for the first time ever, there are no babies. Nobody has given birth. Nobody is expecting. Nobody is waiting to adopt. So the other day, I was thinking. I said to myself, 'Well, Ingeborg, you old silly goose, now what are you going to do with this present?' And I thought about it and thought about it, then I heard you were coming to give me some cookies. And I said to myself, 'Well, Marguerite's has never been in my house before. What could I give her?' So I got the crazy idea that I could give you this. I know you're not a baby, but I thought that maybe you might like it anyway. So here you go."

With that, Ingeborg handed Marguerite the bundle wrapped in white tissue paper and tied with red embroidery floss. Slowly, almost nervously, Marguerite opened the package. It was a beautiful receiving blanket with a cross-stitch picture and a verse in deep reds and blues all framed in magnificent embroidered lace.

Marguerite stammered, "I don't understand."

Ingeborg giggled. "You silly, there's nothing to understand. It's a gift, that's all. See, I put your name in the middle there."

Marguerite took the blanket in her hands and read the words stitched into its very center, "Marguerite Christina Oland, child of God, you have been sealed by the Holy Spirit and marked with the cross of Christ forever." For the first time in her life, Marguerite was speechless.

Ingeborg continued, "I've been thinking a lot about that blanket, it being a receiving blanket and all. I've twisted it around almost every way in my mind. First, I thought about the Christmas verse where it says, 'And the Word became flesh and dwelt among us.' And then it says something like, 'and as many as received him he gave the power to become the children of God.'

"*Well, that's good,* I thought. So when we see one of these blankets, then we can get our hearts ready to receive the Christ Child. You know, to make sure we make a place for him in our lives. So in one way, it's like the blanket is for Jesus.

"But then I thought it works the other way too. Like that verse says, we 'become the children of God.' So then it's like the blanket is for us, to remind us that we are God's children. It probably never happens to you, what with you doing all that stuff at the church and being so important and all. But sometimes, I do something wrong, or it seems like people don't appreciate me, or I just start to feel kind of blue. That's when I need to be reminded that I am God's child. Like that blanket is God's love, and it wraps us up all warm and safe in his love."

Marguerite smiled. She knew exactly what Ingeborg meant.

The smile was all the encouragement Ingeborg needed to finish her little speech. "I guess there's just one more thing about those blankets. Like I said, it reminds me that I'm God's child. That feels good, but I guess it also reminds me that I ought to act like I'm God's child. There's a responsibility that comes with being God's child. There are a lot of people out there who don't have a warm, safe place to go. I guess that blanket reminds me that some people may need me to be that warm, safe place. Sometimes, I need to be a kind of receiving blanket for the people suffering out there."

Marguerite picked up the blanket and rubbed it against her cheek. It did make her feel warm and safe. She didn't like to admit it, but sometimes she did need to feel warm and safe. Like when she lost her position in the circle or when they vetoed her holiday ham loaf or when they didn't want her to speak at the Christmas party.

Marguerite stood up and kissed Ingeborg on the cheek. "Thank you so much for the present. It's the best Christmas gift I've ever received." Then Marguerite left before either she or Ingeborg said something stupid.

Ingeborg didn't know it, but on that afternoon, the most beautiful receiving blanket in the county wasn't tucked under Marguerite's arm. The most beautiful receiving blanket in the county was sitting right there in the front room of that old farmhouse in an automatic lift chair, crocheting an afghan and humming a little Christmas carol as she prepared her heart for the coming of the Christ Child. Marguerite knew how hard it was to find a place that was safe and warm and she said a little prayer thanking God for this wonderful gift, a receiving blanket made of flesh and blood, knit by nothing less than the hands of God.

Connie Bartz: Wounded Healer

December 25, 1999

It all started the Monday before Thanksgiving. Lyle Hegland, the custodian at the Pleasant View Lutheran, and Pastor Michael Loeson were cleaning the sanctuary, getting ready for Thanksgiving Eve worship. Every year at Thanksgiving, the people of Pleasant View turn their sanctuary into a kind of gigantic cornucopia. On Monday they haul in shocks of corn; cupboards full of home-canned goodies in mason jars; and bushel baskets full of apples, squash, and pumpkins. On Tuesday, Marguerite Oland, former chair and present spiritual advisor of the Christian Martyrs Circle, plants herself in the middle of the sanctuary and tells *everyone* where *everything* goes.

On Monday, Pastor Loeson was standing on the altar, dusting the four-foot plaster statue of Christ, when he discovered that the statue of Christ could be moved. At that very moment, he

126

had what he thought was one of the best ideas of his ministry. He immediately asked Lyle to help him move the statue. Lyle refused. He wasn't about to end a thirty-year career as a custodian by removing a perfectly healthy Jesus from his assigned position. What's more, on a less pious note, Marguerite would kill him. Somehow Pastor Loeson managed to get the statue down and hidden behind the door in the sacristy. He went straight to work, and I have to admit, when he was finished, the altar looked magnificent. From the shelf where once Jesus stood, a shiny gold cloth flowed out onto the altar. On top of the cloth lay a handsome wicker basket turned on its side. Out of the basket, great sheaves of wheat and plump bunches of grapes tumbled down onto the altar. On the altar, in the middle of the grapes and wheat, stood the Communion elements: a brilliant silver chalice and a buttery brown loaf of homemade bread.

Tuesday night was a bit of a disappointment. Unbeknownst to Pastor Loeson, the Sassy Sixties Senior Society had chartered a bus to the casino just outside of Watertown. Nearly the whole town went, so that the only ones who showed up were Pastor Loeson, Lyle, Marguerite, and Connie Bartz.

Now, in the words of Marguerite Oland, Connie was a bit slow. She and her mother lived across the section north of church. Her mother divided her time between Four Corners Hardware where she worked as a clerk and The Highway Tap where she fed her craving for Lucky Strikes and Four Roses. That left Connie to fend for herself. Connie got around on an old blue Schwinn Hollywood bicycle. She was as strong as an ox and had an incredible appetite, so she went anywhere that food would be served. She never missed a wedding dance, a church social, or a funeral for that matter. Most of the time she hung out at Betty's

Ceramic Shop where she helped Betty move and paint the heavy stuff in exchange for chocolate chip cookies.

Tuesday night, Connie was the first one at the church because she heard that Marguerite was serving what she claimed to be the best pumpkin bars in South Dakota. She, Lyle, and Pastor Loeson were standing in the front of the church when Marguerite came in. She plopped her picnic basket on the floor, flung her coat in the pew, and turned to face the altar. When she saw the altar, her chin nearly hit the floor. She staggered back against the pew in true biblical flair and said, "Please, sir, where have you taken my Lord?"

The pastor tried to explain the deep symbolism of the display, finishing with a statement something like, "and so if we truly believe in the real presence than indeed Jesus is still there in the bread and the wine."

Marguerite looked at him incredulously and didn't talk to him for the rest of the night. They put things where they belonged, Connie finished off the pumpkin bars, and everyone went home.

Thanksgiving services were abysmal. Pastor Loeson tried to do his best, but it was hard to convey an "attitude of gratitude" with Marguerite Oland glaring at the place where her "beloved Lord and Savior" once stood. After the service, Marguerite met Michael in the center aisle and delivered her ultimatum: "I'm going to Fargo. I'll be back on Christmas Eve. I expect when I return, the Lord will be in his proper place."

Marguerite marched out the back of the church. Pastor Loeson sulked up to the front of the church muttering to himself. He was so distraught that he didn't notice the ear of corn lying on the floor. The corn rolled under his foot, and he was flung against the sacristy door. The door broke his fall when it banged hard against something behind it. That something was the statue of Jesus. With fear and trembling, Pastor Loeson looked behind the door. There stood Marguerite's Lord and Savior, his right arm broken just below the elbow, bent in a very unhealthy angle.

I can't repeat exactly what Pastor Loeson said at that moment. But Connie Bartz can. She was just walking in and heard exactly what he said. She laughed at Pastor Loeson. "You talk like my mom does when she's drinking."

She was about to say something else when a voice from the basement told her to come and have a second piece of pie.

Pastor Loeson and Lyle hid the statue in the boiler room under a paper drum while they tried to figure out how to fix it. Lyle called around, and the only place that could fix it was in Saint Louis. They told him they couldn't get to it for two months, and it would cost $1,800.

On Sunday, Pastor Loeson climbed into the pulpit and complained bitterly about how little time we Americans spend giving thanks. He announced that he had decided to extend the period of Thanksgiving. The rest of the Thanksgiving decorations could go, but his Thanksgiving display on the altar would be staying up indefinitely.

For three weeks, Lyle and the Pastor tried to fix the statue. Lyle tried fixing it with duct tape. It worked, but it made it look like Jesus was suffering from tennis elbow. Michael put a pair of knee-high nylon stockings on Jesus's arms, but it made it look like Jesus had a farmer's tan. They tried draping some Christmas garlands around his back and over both of his arms, but that made him look like he was wearing a green feather boa.

The congregation of Pleasant View Lutheran dearly loved Michael Loeson, but they also loved their statue of Jesus. It was more than a statue to them. It reminded them of God's gift to them. During his sermons, Michael could see members of the congregation looking at the altar with pure Advent piety, longing for Jesus to come again. Pastor Loeson felt the distant hand of Marguerite Oland when the members of the Christian Martyrs Circle, providing special music for the day, chose to stand at the foot of the altar and sing "Come Thou Long Expected Jesus."

Michael couldn't take the pressure. He was desperate to get away, so the Monday before Christmas, he escaped to spend three days making Communion calls. Michael never saw it, but shortly after he left, Connie rode up on her old blue bicycle, wearing a heavy backpack. She went straight to Jesus's hiding place in the basement. On Thursday, Pastor Loeson was sitting at his computer, *not* writing his sermon, when there was a knock at the door. He turned around and there was Connie, covered with paint. She smiled from ear to ear and said, "He's fixed!"

Pastor Loeson looked at her, dumbfounded. "Who's fixed?"

Connie said, "Jesus. I put him back up on the altar. Come see. He looks even better than before!"

With terror in his eyes, Pastor Loeson ran into the church and, sure enough, there was Jesus, right back where he belonged. But he wasn't the same. To be sure, he was fixed. There was no sign of a fracture anywhere to be seen. His skin looked smooth and natural. But that wasn't all. Deep in the palms of his hands and on the tops of his feet and in his side, there were brilliant scarlet wounds. Against the creamy, smooth, unblemished flesh, the wounds looked grotesque.

Connie came and stood beside the pastor and said with a classic Connie Bartz smile,

"I did good, didn't I?"

Pastor Loeson stammered.

Connie continued. "I looked at him real close. The man who made him put scars on his hands and his feet and in his side, but somebody must have painted over them. Somebody didn't want us to see Jesus's wounds. Somebody wanted him to look pretty. But that's lying. I put the wounds back. I want him to look real."

Pastor Loeson climbed up onto the altar. Sure enough, there were wounds sculpted into the plaster. At some point, they had been painted over. He could see how Connie had carefully blended the paint and brought the wounds to life. Michael turned and looked down at her with amazement. She was looking intently at her hands, trying to rub the paint off them. In the dim light, the red paint on her hands made it look like Connie herself was wounded. Considering her life, I suppose she was. In a way, I supposed Pastor Loeson was wounded too. In a way, I suppose we all are.

In the thirty seconds that Michael Loeson stood there looking at Connie, his Christmas sermon wrote itself. I can't repeat to you word for word what he said, but I can tell you the gist of it. On Christmas Eve, the members of the congregation flooded into the sanctuary, each looking in shocked amazement at the statue of the bleeding Christ. With the candles flickering on the Advent wreath, Pastor Loeson climbed into the pulpit. He turned and looked at the wounded Jesus standing over the altar, his arms outstretched, his eyes gazing lovingly at the baby in the manger. He turned and looked at the congregation, their faces uplifted. Some of them were gazing at the manger where, at last, the Christ Child had come. Some of them were gazing at the altar where, at last, their blessed Savior had returned.

He told them the whole story about the broken Messiah. He told them about the broken pastor who tried to hide his sin. He told them about the wonderful broken woman named Connie who was so bold as to touch Jesus with healing hands and to lovingly reveal our Savior's wounds.

And then he said something like this:

"This year, we have observed a true Advent season. Over the past weeks, we have been waiting—waiting for our Jesus to come back to us. We really wanted Jesus to come to us in pristine condition—without a scratch, without a blemish. But what we got is not what we expected. What we got is a Jesus who is broken and wounded.

"Christmas is a strange time. It is the season when we celebrate God's coming to live among us. We spend weeks preparing for the coming of Jesus. We sing songs of longing for the beauty of God's salvation. But when he finally comes, we are surprised. He is not what we expect. We expect a beautiful little baby born in perfect circumstances that will take away all the messiness of this life. But what we get is a child born in the coarseness of a stable. His impoverished parents are driven from their home by an infant-murdering king. He is rejected by all of those who claim to know the ways of God. He socializes with the crudest of society, and in the end, he hangs on the cross—broken, despised, rejected, and wounded. A man more than a little acquainted with grief."

'And by his stripes we are healed.'

"You see, we don't need a beautiful baby. We don't need a messiah with his wounds painted over. We need a god who will wade into our broken and wounded world and hold us in our brokenness, woundedness, and sinfulness. We don't need a pretty Jesus. We need a real Jesus who will give us the courage to uncover our own wounds, our own brokenness, our own sinfulness so that we can be healed and so that we can reach out with healing hands to the broken and wounded around us. That is what Christmas is about. That is what our God is about."

Pastor Loeson took his seat, and Kimberly Johnson, home from school at Augustana, in a special arrangement written for alto voice and violin, sang these words.

> He was despised and rejected of men:
> A man of sorrows, and acquainted with grief.
> Surely he hath borne our griefs,
> And carried our sorrows;
> He was wounded for our transgressions;
> He was bruised for our iniquities;
> The chastisement of our peace was upon him.
> And with his stripes we are healed.

Connie Bartz is riding a new bike these days. It's a beautiful red one with knobby tires and twenty-one speeds. It showed up at her house the day after Christmas. There wasn't a card or anything saying from whom it came from. There were just two bags hanging from the handlebars. One was full of the most delicious pumpkin bars in all South Dakota, and the other was stuffed with plump bunches of purple grapes and a buttery loaf of home-baked bread.